AF609259

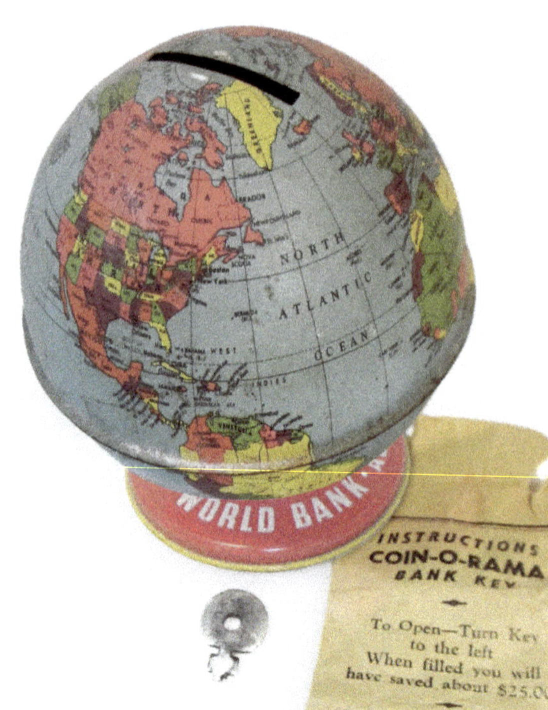

NORTH
ATLANTIC
OCEAN
WORLD BANK
INSTRUCTIONS
COIN-O-RAMA
BANK KEY
To Open—Turn Key
to the left
When filled you will
have saved about $25.00
Deposit contents to your
account regularly-then watch
your savings grow.

CAPITAL OF THE WORLD

Rob Kovitz

Treyf Books
Keep Refrigerated

Published by Treyf Books
5-193 Furby Street
Winnipeg, MB Canada R3C 2A6
www.treyf.com
keeprefrigerated@treyf.com

A version of this project was first published in
Scapegoat 04: Currency, Winter/Spring 2013.

LIBRARY AND ARCHIVES CANADA CATALOGUING IN PUBLICATION

Kovitz, Rob, 1963-, author, artist
Capital of the world / by Rob Kovitz.

Includes bibliographical references.
Issued in print and electronic formats.
ISBN 978-1-927923-05-4 (pbk.).
ISBN 978-1-927923-06-1 (epub).
ISBN 978-1-927923-07-8 (pdf)

1. Kovitz, Rob, 1963-. 2. Artists' books--Canada. I. Title.

N7433.4.K68C36 2014 700.971 C2013-908423-1
C2013-908424-X

Financial assistance for the creation and production of Treyf Books is sometimes provided by the Canada Council for the Arts, the Manitoba Arts Council, and the City of Winnipeg through the Winnipeg Arts Council.

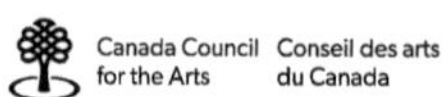

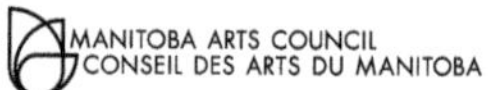

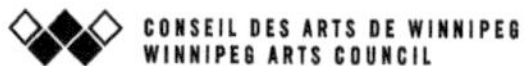

10 9 8 7 6 5 4 3 2 1

LEGAL INFO: FAIR USE NOTICE

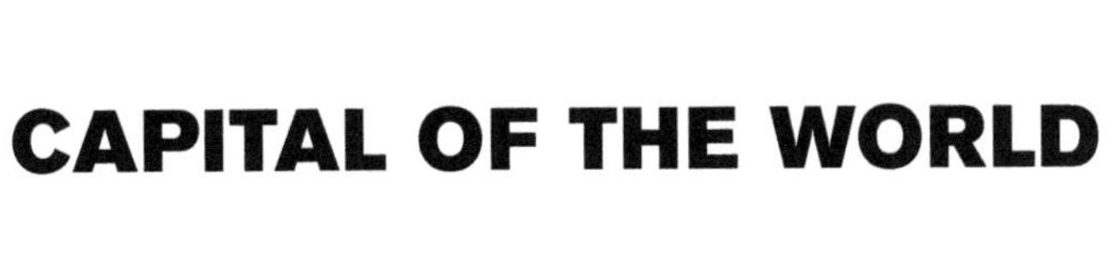
CAPITAL OF THE WORLD

It was he who broached the question of money, like a solicitor discussing a client's case.

Émile Zola, *The Kill*

Possibly because I was born into what in America fits the description of a privileged class, I'm hard put to pretend that it doesn't exist. So would have been America's Founding Fathers, almost all of them men of property setting up a government hospitable to the acquisition of more property. Unlike the Magna Carta, the Constitution doesn't contemplate the sharing of the commons inherent in a bountiful wilderness; it provides the means of making manifest an unequal division of the spoils. Thomas Jefferson didn't confuse the theory—"All men are created equal"—with the practice—"Money, not morality, is the principle of commercial nations."

Lewis H. Lapham, *Ignorance of Things Past*

'Ah, excellent, excellent, I must send that to the papers tomorrow.'

'You're quite right, Messieurs, we live in good times,' said Mignon, by way of summing up, in the midst of the smiles and approving remarks provoked by the Baron's epigram. 'I know quite a few who have done very well out of it. You see, everything seems fine when you're making money.'

Émile Zola, *The Kill*

Which is to say, a government of the rich, by the rich, and for the rich—Obama beholden to Goldman Sachs and JPMorgan Chase, Romney risen from the black lagoon of Bain Capital. The news is maybe unwelcome, but it doesn't come as a surprise. Where in the record books does one look for a government of the poor, by the poor, and for the poor? How else does a society know or govern itself if not with guidelines shaped by some form of class distinction? In the United States the table of organization is for sale, made with money instead of an aristocratic birthright, the favor of a king, or the grace of God.

Lewis H. Lapham, *Ignorance of Things Past*

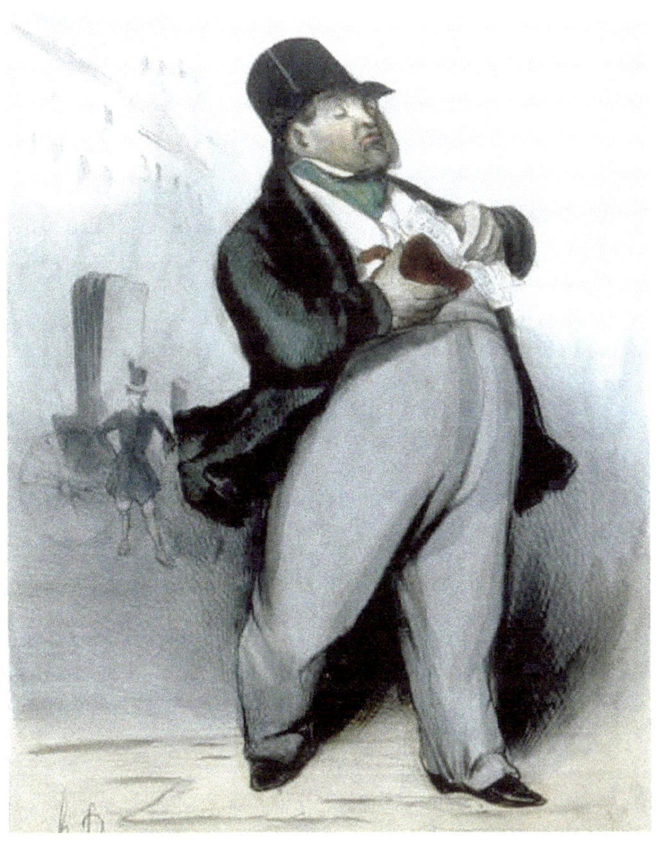

The Banker. Called *financial capacity* because he is nothing but a recipient, a coffer exclusively fit for finances.

Honoré Daumier, *Le Charivari,* 16 October 1835

After the July-Revolution of 1835 the banker Lafitte is seen showing the Duc d'Orléans into City Hall. At this occasion he meaningfully said: "From now on the bankers will run the country!"

Dieter Noack and Lilian Noack, *The Daumier Register*

All this time Monsieur Toutin-Laroche, who had been interrupted, was holding forth, as if he were delivering a peroration amid the attentive silence of the City Council:

'The results are superb. This City loan will be remembered as one of the finest financial operations of the age. Yes, Messieurs!'

Émile Zola, *The Kill*

At no point in its history has the country not been nailed to a cross of gold. Mark Hanna, the Ohio coal merchant managing William McKinley's presidential campaign against William Jennings Bryan in 1896, phrased the proposition in a form that our own cable-channel commentariat still plays as late-breaking news: "There are two things that are important in politics. The first is money, and I can't remember what the second one is." The Supreme Court in 2010 sustained the judgment with the *Citizens United* ruling that deregulated the market in political office and thus ratified the opinion of John Jay, appointed chief justice in 1789, that "those who own the country ought to govern it."

Lewis H. Lapham, *Ignorance of Things Past*

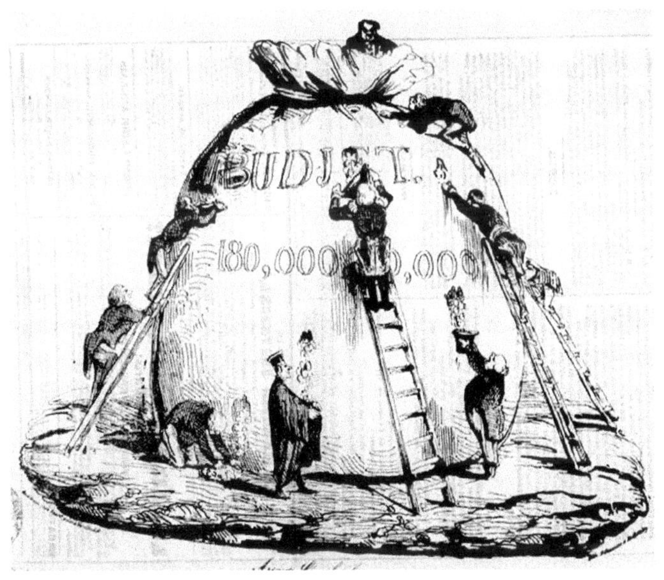

Legislative assault.

Honoré Daumier, *Le Charivari,* 30 May 1835

Judges, officers and other members of the government are depleting the budget of France by digging holes in the huge bag of money. The ministers are helping themselves in a very personal way to funds from the state budget.

In April/May 1835, the annual budget discussions took place (see also DR 237). In its edition of May 30, 1835, the *Charivari* cynically remarked that "the same people who vote for the budget are the ones who will be devouring it".

Dieter Noack and Lilian Noack, *The Daumier Register*

'You're too kind; we just did our job.'

But Charrier was not so clumsy. He drank his glass of Pomard and managed to deliver himself of a sentence:

'The changes in Paris', he said, 'have given the working man a living.'

'And we can add,' resumed Monsieur Toutin-Laroche, 'that they have given a tremendous boost to finance and industry.'

'Don't forget the artistic side: the new boulevards are quite majestic,' added Monsieur Hupel de la Noue, who prided himself on his taste.

'Yes, yes, it's all quite wonderful,' murmured Monsieur de Mareuil for the sake of saying something.

'As to the cost,' declared Haffner, the deputy who never opened his mouth except on great occasions, 'that will be for our children to bear, nothing could be fairer.'

As he said this, he looked at Monsieur de Saffré, who appeared to have given momentary offence to the pretty Madame Michelin, and the young secretary, to show that he had been following the conversation, repeated:

'Nothing could be fairer indeed.'

Émile Zola, *The Kill*

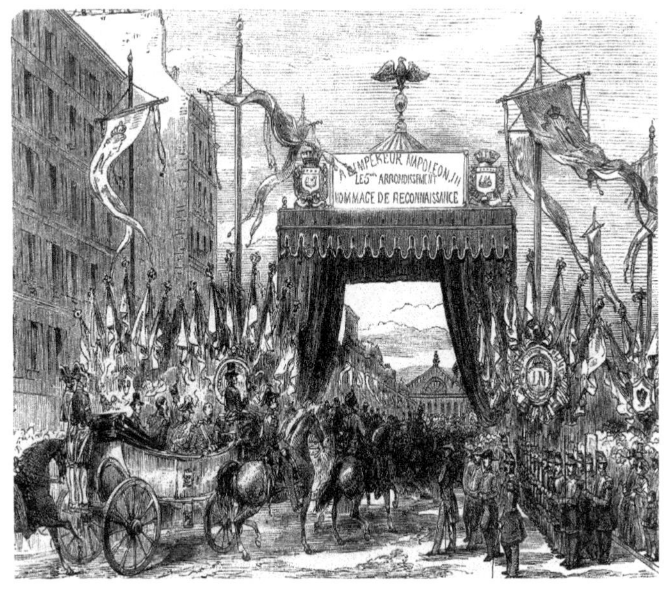

Inauguration du boulevard de Strasbourg, le dix Décembre 1853

Napoleon III appointed the Baron Haussmann in 1852 to modernize Paris and to create new avenues and boulevards. This print dates from a year later, and represents the inauguration of the boulevard de Strasbourg, which is to this date one of the major streets in the 10th arrondissement of Paris.

Brown University Library, *Paris: Capital of the 19th Century*

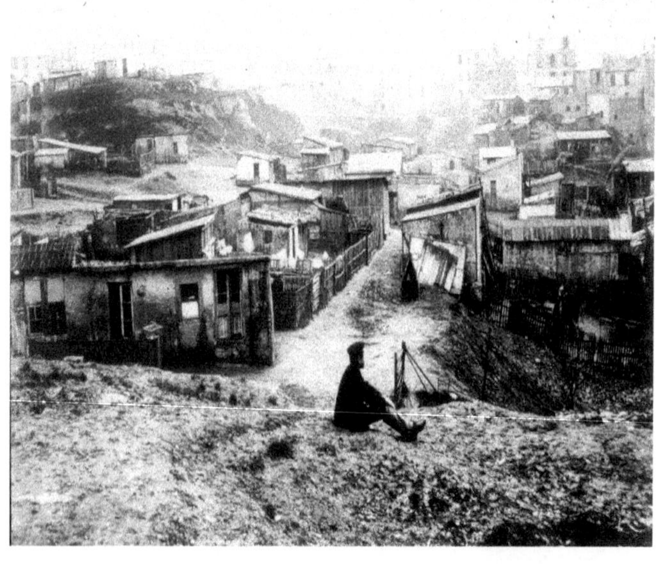

Charles Marville, *Slums: Haut de la Rue Champlain,* 1860

The development and urbanization of Paris under Haussmann contributed to a major increase in rent in the newly renovated quarters. As a result, many working-class families were forced to emigrate to the exterior of the city. Haussmann's Paris was thus "divided" into a bourgeois center surrounded by working-class suburbs.

Brown University Library, *Paris: Capital of the 19th Century*

Nor at any point in its history has America declared a lasting peace between the haves and the have-nots. Temporary cessations of hostilities, but no permanent closing of the moral and social gap between debtor and creditor. Dipped at birth in the font of boom and bust, the United States over the past 225 years has suffered the embarrassment of multiple bank panics and collapses into economic recession. The worst of the consequences invariably accrue to the accounts defaulting on the loans of bourgeois respectability, the would-be upwardly mobile poor taking the fall for their betters.

The notion of a classless society derives its credibility from the relatively few periods in the life of the nation during which circumstances allowed for social readjustment and experiment—in the 1830s, '40s, and '50s, again in the 1950s and '60s—but for the most part the record will show the game securely rigged in favor of the rich, no matter how selfish or stupid, at the expense of the poor, no matter how innovative or entrepreneurial.

A democratic society puts a premium on equality; a capitalist economy does not. Inequality—buy cheap, sell dear—is for capitalism the name of the game.

Lewis H. Lapham, *Ignorance of Things Past*

But Monsieur Toutin-Laroche was not a man to lose his train of thought.

'Ah! Messieurs,' he continued when the laughter had subsided, 'yesterday was a great consolation to us, since our administration is exposed to such base attacks. They accuse the Council of leading the City to destruction, and you see, no sooner does the City issue a loan than they all bring us their money, even those who complain.'

'You've worked wonders,' said Saccard. 'Paris has become the capital of the world.'

'Yes, it's quite amazing,' interjected Monsieur Hupel de la Noue. 'Just imagine! I've lived in Paris all my life, and I don't know the city any more. I got lost yesterday on my way from the Hôtel de Ville to the Luxembourg. It's amazing, quite amazing!'

There was a pause. Everyone was listening now.

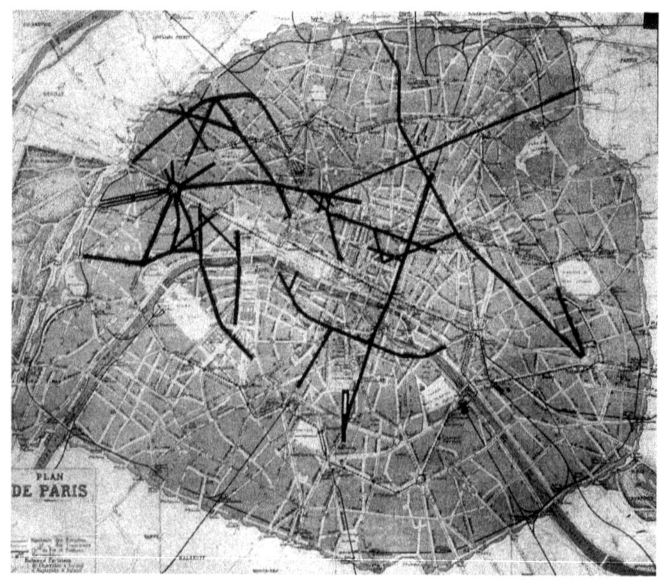

Haussmann's Plan with Boulevards, ca. 1860

Brown University Library, *Paris: Capital of the 19th Century*

... Baron Georges-Eugène Haussmann [(h)OHSS-mahn] (1809-1891), inventor of the modern city. Haussmann was appointed by Emperor Napoleon III (Bonaparte's nephew), who wanted an opulent imperial capital and an efficient center of modern commerce and industry. The emperor also wanted a seat of government secure from the French capital's habitual political uprisings.

To build the straight new boulevards, Haussmann plowed through traditional neighborhoods, demolishing some 12,000 buildings, including many homes of the poor and working classes. He lined his boulevards with uniform, fashionable apartment buildings and punctuated his streets with broad plazas, where Parisians could stroll and play. In all, Paris gained some 95 miles (150 km) of new streets and a feeling of spaciousness and regularity. Not surprisingly, Hausmann's Paris was best suited to the city's affluent middle class, who enjoyed fashionable housing, parks for their leisure, and a chance to profit in Hausmann's complicated financial schemes ...

Philip E. Bishop, *Adventures in the Human Spirit*

'The transformation of Paris', continued Monsieur Toutin Laroche, 'will be the glory of the Empire. The nation is ungrateful; it ought to kiss the Emperor's feet. As I said this morning in the Council meeting, when we were discussing the success of the loan: "Gentlemen, let that rabble of an Opposition say what they like; to turn Paris upside-down is to make it productive."'

Saccard smiled and closed his eyes, as if to savour the sublety of the epigram.

Émile Zola, *The Kill*

Paris at that time was a fascinating spectacle for a man like Aristide Saccard. The Empire had just been proclaimed, after the famous journey in the course of which the Prince-President had succeeded in stirring up the enthusiasm of a few Bonapartist departments. The Chamber and the press were silent. Society, saved once again, congratulated itself and relaxed now that it had a strong government to protect it and relieve it of the trouble of thinking for itself and looking after its own affairs. The main preoccupation of society was to know how to enjoy itself. In Eugène Rougon's happy phrase, Paris had sat down to dinner and was wondering how to take its pleasure after dessert. Politics terrified it, like a dangerous drug. Men's enervated minds turned towards dissipation and speculation. Those who had money brought it forth from its hiding-place, and those who had none looked for forgotten treasures in every nook and cranny. And underneath the turmoil there was a subdued quiver, a nascent sound of five-franc pieces, of women's rippling laughter, and the still faint clatter of plates and the sound of kisses. In the midst of the great silence, the absolute peace of the new reign of order, there arose every kind of salacious rumour, every kind of golden and voluptuous promise. It was as if one were passing by one of those little houses whose closely drawn curtains reveal only women's shadows, and from which no sound issues but that of gold coins on the marble mantelpieces. The Empire was on the point of turning Paris into the bawdy house of Europe. The gang of fortune-seekers who had succeeded in stealing a throne required a reign of adventures, shady transactions, sold consciences, bought women,

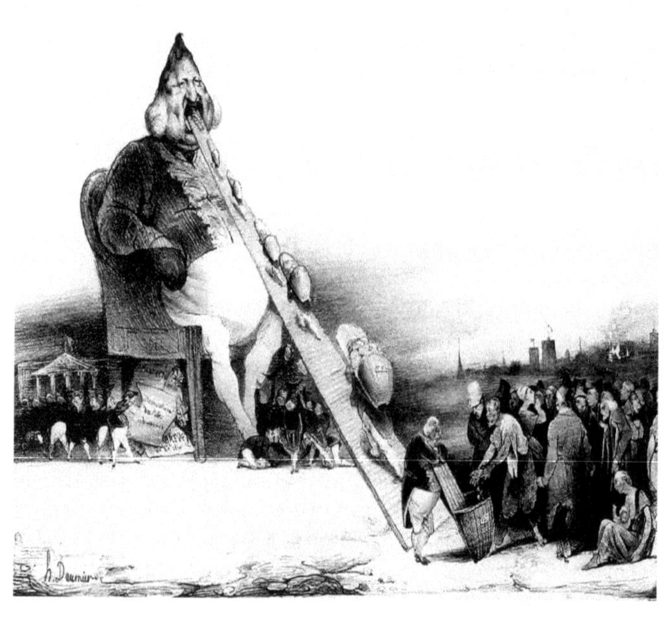

Gargantua.

Honoré Daumier, *La Caricature,* 16 December 1831

Gargantua represents Louis-Philippe seated on his throne and swallowing bags of coins which have been extracted from the poor by his ministers and which are carried by lilliputian personnages up a plank that stretches from the ground to his mouth. At the foot of the plank is a crowd of miserable men and women handing over their money. About the throne are fat little favourites gathering up peerages, decorations, commissions, and the like, into which the enforced offerings have been converted.

Dieter Noack and Lilian Noack, *The Daumier Register*

and rampant drunkenness. In the city where the blood of December had hardly been washed away, there sprang up, timidly as yet, the mad desire for dissipation that was destined to drag the country down to the level of the most decadent and dishonoured of nations.

From the beginning Aristide Saccard could sense the rising tide of speculation, which was soon to engulf the whole of Paris. He watched its progress intently. He found himself in the midst of the hot rain of crown-pieces that fell thickly on the city's roofs. In his endless wanderings through the corridors of the Hôtel de Ville, he had got wind of the vast project for the transformation of Paris, the plan for the demolitions, the new boulevards and neighbourhoods, the huge piece of jobbery in the sale of land and property, which throughout the city was beginning to ignite the conflict of interests and the blaze of unrestrained luxury. Now his activity had a purpose. It was during this period that he developed his geniality. He even put on a little weight and stopped hurrying through the streets like a scrawny cat looking for food. At his office he was more chatty and obliging than ever. His brother, whom he visited in a more or less official manner, complimented him on putting his advice so happily into practice. Early in 1854 Saccard confided to him that he had several pieces of business in view, but that he would require a rather large advance.

'Look for it,' said Eugène.

'You're quite right, I'll look for it,' he replied good-humouredly, appearing not to notice that his brother had just refused to provide him with the initial capital.

The thought of this capital now obsessed him. His plan was formed; it matured day by day. But the first few thousand francs were not to be found. He became more and more tense; he looked at passers-by in a nervous, searching manner as if life were seeking a lender in every wayfarer. At home Angèle continued to lead her modest and contented existence. He waited for his opportunity; and his genial laughter became more bitter as this opportunity failed to present itself.

Émile Zola, *The Kill*

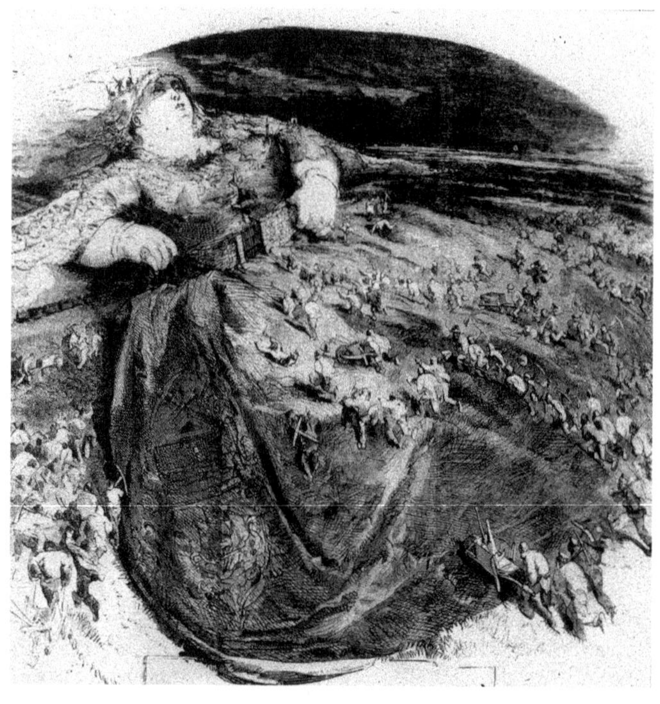

Edmont Morin, *Caricature of Paris Invaded by Demolishers*

While Haussmann is often credited for the "charm" of Paris as we know it today, urbanization of the city depended on the demolition and destruction of many residential properties and traditional quarters. Haussmann's work was therefore the inspiration for a variety of satirical and political cartoons during the Second Empire, many of which personified Paris as feminine. Edmont Morin's caricature emphasizes the invasive and destructive nature of Haussmann's demolition team.

Brown University Library, *Paris: Capital of the 19th Century*

Even a monkey can make money. That's what my mother always told me, but I think she undersold herself. She was a remarkable woman. That's why I'm remarking on her now. She was also the only person who ever seemed like a person to me.

She started out like everybody else, if everybody else started out as a half-cultured girl from Connecticut who reckoned that all she had to do was sustain an aura of dazzling freshness and a husband would arrive to keep her in cozy bondage. She'd raise some love-starved children, and the husband would bring home the bacon and, with any luck, not spend many waking hours at home, eating it.

This is exactly how it went for a while, but then her particular bacon-procurer drove home from the city dead drunk and died. So she went out and made her own, well, let's just call it money, again. My mother became a successful Realtor, and invested in many soon-to-be-lucrative areas early. But her stock-market strategies aren't the point. The fact that here was a woman, a nearly destitute widow, in a very sexist America, who ventured out into a man's world and amazed is the point. I grew up rich, and she sent me to top-shelf schools. I took art history, and some art-theory classes that puzzled and intrigued me. There was the funny lingo. Everybody was always "interrogating hegemonic discourse" and so forth. I hung out with kids who were really fascinated by this crap.

Sam Lipsyte, *The Republic of Empathy*

Over the last thirty years, the university has replaced the labor union as the most important institution, after the corporation, in American political and economic life. As union jobs have disappeared, participation in the labor force, the political system, and cultural affairs is increasingly regulated by professional guilds that require their members to spend the best years of life paying exorbitant tolls and kissing patrician rings. Whatever modest benefits accreditation offers in signaling attainment of skills, as a ranking mechanism it's zero-sum: the result is to enrich the accreditors and to discredit those who lack equivalent credentials.

Jean Baudrillard once suggested an important correction to classical Marxism: exchange value is not, as Marx had it, a distortion of a commodity's underlying use value; use value, instead, is a fiction created by exchange value. In the same way, systems of accreditation do not assess merit; merit is a fiction created by systems of accreditation. Like the market for skin care products, the market for credentials is inexhaustible: as the bachelor's degree becomes democratized, the master's degree becomes mandatory for advancement. Our elaborate, expensive system of higher education is first and foremost a system of stratification, and only secondly—and very dimly—a system for imparting knowledge.

The original universities in the Western world organized themselves as guilds, either of students, as in Bologna, or of masters, as in Paris. From the first, their chief mission was to produce not learning but graduates, with teaching subordinated to the process of certification—much as artisans would impose long and wasteful periods of apprenticeship, under the guise of "training," to keep their numbers scarce and their services expensive. For the contemporary bachelor or master or doctor of this or that, as for the Ming-era scholar–bureaucrat or the medieval European guildsman, income and social position are acquired through affiliation with a cartel. Those who want to join have to pay to play, and many never recover from the entry fee.

n+1 Magazine, *Death by Degrees*

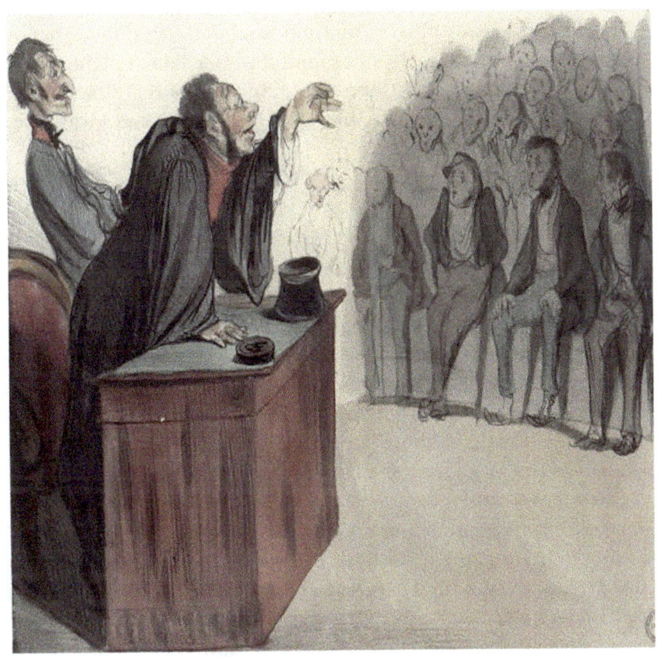

Robert Macaire, Professor of Industry.

Here's an example. Buy a new process, it doesn't matter which, or whether it's good or bad, buy it for 600F, 500F, 25F, for as little as possible. Create 500'000F worth of shares, as many as possible. Make out monster advertisements, monster posters, monster promises. Make the capital, pocket it, put the key under the door, file your bankruptcy papers, that's to say the company's papers ... that's the end of that little game. You then go on to another.

Honoré Daumier, *Le Charivari*, 29 January 1837

They were also really into cocaine and sex. I was bound for an M.B.A. after college, but I liked to sit around the table late at night, drunk and high, smoking cigarettes and arguing points that I had barely grasped in seminar. I usually brought the cocaine, and I was often rewarded with sex.

Sam Lipsyte, *The Republic of Empathy*

Of course, one man's burden is another man's opportunity. Student debt in the United States now exceeds $1 trillion. Like cigarette duties or state lotteries, debt-financed accreditation functions as a tax on the poor. But whereas sin taxes at least subsidize social spending, the "graduation tax" is doubly regressive, transferring funds from the young and poor to the old and affluent. The accreditors do well, and the creditors do even better. Student-loan asset-backed securities are far safer than their more famous cousins in the mortgage market: the government guarantees most of the liability, and, crucially, student loans cannot be erased by declaring bankruptcy. Although America's college graduates are already late on paying nearly $300 billion in loans, they don't have the option of walking away from these debts, even if their careers have been effectively transformed into underwater assets.

As the credentialism compulsion seeps down the socioeconomic ladder, universities jack up fees and taxi drivers hire $200-an-hour SAT tutors for their children. The collective impact may be ruinous, but for individuals the outlays seem justified. As a consequence, college tuitions are nowhere near their limit; as long as access to the workforce is controlled by the bachelor's degree, students will pay more and more.

n+1 Magazine, *Death by Degrees*

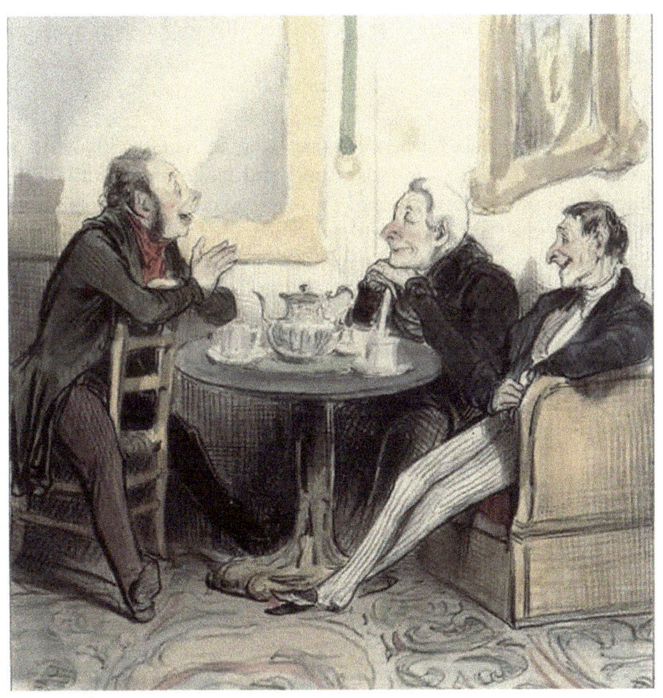

The other day, I pulled off another smart trick ... I had set up a firm with a capital of ten million francs to exploit top boots in cardboard ... I had placed only eight shares worth a petty 1200 francs ... I called together my eight shareholders and held forth in something like the following manner: "Ah! Good-day ye strolling gentlemen, how handsome you are, how fine you seem!" I promised them more cheese than bread, I gave them a 50% dividend, I warmed them up a bit and let them simmer ... The following day they couldn't get hold of my shares fast enough, I placed all of them and at the next meeting I said: "The last time I did the books I made a mistake. I forgot to take into account the price of the cardboard and its fabrication. You must return the dividend I gave you, I'm going to hold it back ... I put down nothing and kept back the rest. Ha! Ha! Ha! (laughed Bertrand)—He! He! He! (laughed Wormspire.)

Honoré Daumier, *Le Charivari,* 15 November 1838

'Please,' he said, 'let us hear no more of this unpleasant question of money.'

Émile Zola, *The Kill*

I forgot most of this for many years. I went into banking and made mad cake. I managed a hedge fund and made madder cake, or, rather, money. I became one of those guys you never see and have never heard of but who are the sick-ass kings of certain sectors of the market, employing instruments you could never in your math-illiterate lifetime comprehend. I know this tone, my tone, is insufferable. But that's the thing that nobody understands. If you want to make money, you have to be smart and an asshole and also work harder than anyone else. Most people can't manage all three. But I could, and I prospered, as my mother had.

Sam Lipsyte, *The Republic of Empathy*

'Dear lady, have we not said enough, need we continue to talk of this confounded money? Please listen, I want to tell you everything about myself because I would be most unhappy if I failed to earn your respect. I lost my wife recently, I have two children on my hands, and I'm a sensible, practical man. By marrying your niece I am doing good all round. If you still have any reservations about me, you will lose them later on when I've dried everyone's tears and made a fortune for the whole family. Success is a golden flame that purifies everything ...'

Émile Zola, *The Kill*

His plan for making a fortune was simple and practical. Now that he had at his disposal more money than he had ever hoped for to begin his operations, he intended to put his schemes into action on a large scale. He had the whole of Paris at his fingertips; he knew that the shower of gold beating down upon the walls would fall more heavily every day. Smart people had merely to open their pockets. He had joined the clever ones by reading the future in the offices of the Hôtel de Ville. His duties had taught him what can be stolen in the buying and selling of houses and land. He was well versed in every

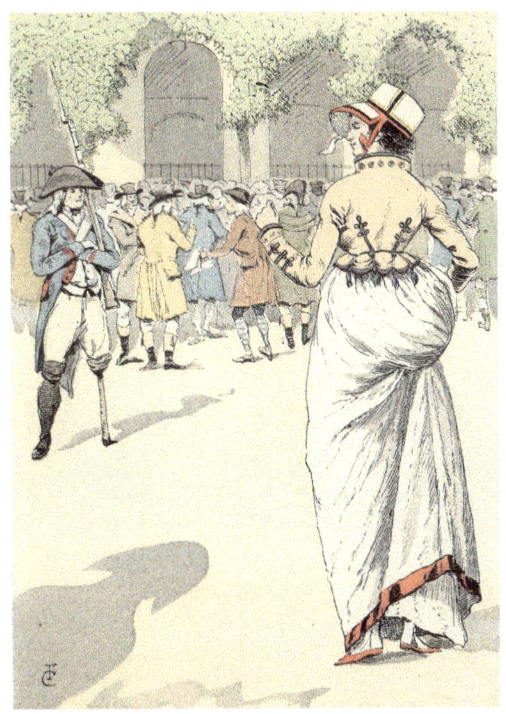

François Courboin, *Stock-Jobbing In The Palais-Royal*

A woman is depicted waiting outside of a group of men, guarded by a one-legged soldier. As the description says, they are stock-jobbing, or buying and selling speculative stocks, with little regard for the value of the capital of the company, simply to make a fast and easy profit. This practice was popularized in the 18th century by the English bourgeois. The woman wears a fitted coat, resembling a man's English hunting coat. At this period, London was increasingly the center of men's fashion, as manifested by its influence on the still-dominant Parisian women's fashion. This women's dress is somewhat frillier and wider than the neo-classical 'chemise,' as women's dresses became more ornate as the 19th century progressed.

Octave Uzanne, *Fashion in Paris: The Various Phases of Feminine Taste and Aesthetics From 1797 to 1897 (London: William Heinemann,* 1898)

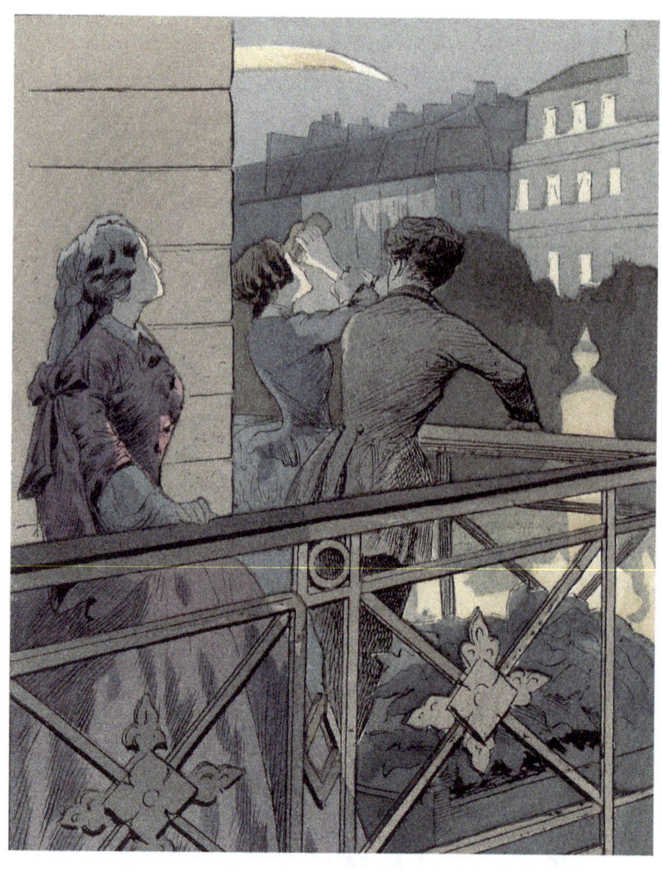

François Courboin, *Watching the Comet on the Boulevards*, 1857

The people depicted in this plate are observing the comet from a balcony typical of the kind of building constructed along Haussman's boulevards. The man is dressed in a black evening costume. The woman in the foreground wears a wide, brightly colored dress supported by a crinoline.

Octave Uzanne, *Fashion in Paris: The Various Phases of Feminine Taste and Aesthetics From 1797 to 1897 (London: William Heinemann,* 1898)

classical swindle: he knew how you sell for a million what has cost you a hundred thousand francs; how you acquire the right to rifle the treasury of the State, which smiles and closes its eyes; how, when throwing a boulevard across the belly of an old neighbourhood, you juggle with six-storeyed houses to the unanimous applause of your dupes. In these still uncertain days, when the disease of speculation was still in its period of incubation, what made him a formidable gambler was that he saw further than his superiors into the stone-and-plaster future reserved for Paris. He had ferreted so much, collected so many clues, that he could have prophesied how the new neighbourhoods would look in 1870. Sometimes, in the street, he would look curiously at certain houses, as if they were acquaintances whose destiny, known to him alone, deeply affected him.

Émile Zola, *The Kill*

His eyes constantly returned, lovingly, to the living, seething ocean from which issued the deep voice of the crowd. It was autumn; beneath the pale sky the city lay listless in a soft and tender grey, pierced here and there by dark patches of foliage that resembled the broad leaves of water-lilies floating on a lake; the sun was setting behind a red cloud and, while the background was filled with a light haze, a shower of gold dust, of golden dew, fell on the right bank of the river, near the Madeleine and the Tuileries. It was like an enchanted corner in a city of the 'Arabian Nights', with emerald trees, sapphire roofs, and ruby weathercocks. At one moment a ray of sunlight gliding from between two clouds was so resplendent that the houses seemed to catch fire and melt like an ingot of gold in a crucible.

'Oh! Look!' said Saccard, laughing like a child. 'It's raining twenty-franc pieces in Paris!'

Émile Zola, *The Kill*

OXFORD WORLD'S CLASSICS

ÉMILE ZOLA

THE KILL

A new translation by Brian Nelson

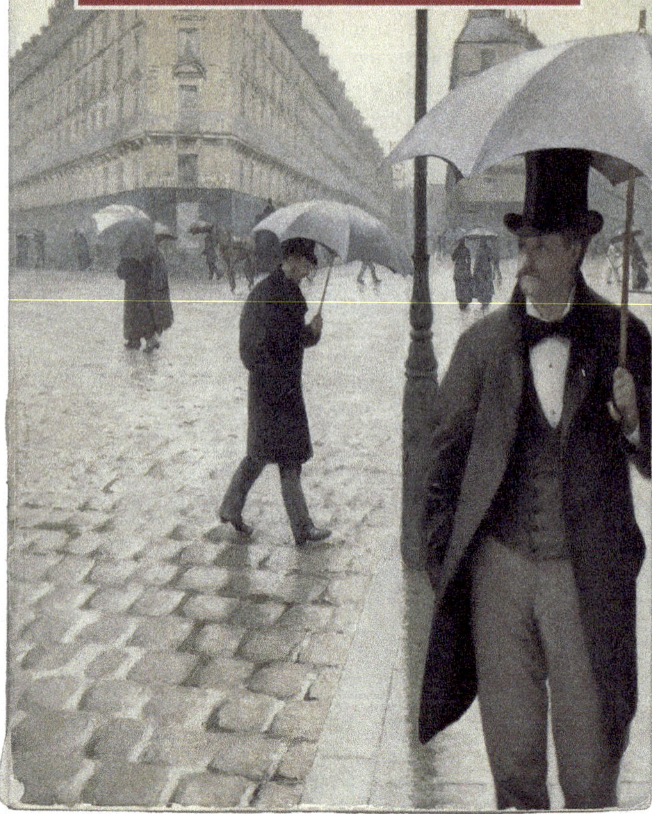

Aristide Saccard was in his element at last. He had shown himself to be a great speculator, capable of making millions. After the master-stroke in the Rue de la Pépinière, he threw himself boldly into the struggle which was beginning to fill Paris with shameful disasters and overnight triumphs. He began by gambling on certainties, repeating his first success, buying up houses which he knew to be threatened with demolition, and using his friends to obtain huge compensation prices. The moment came when he had five or six houses, the same houses he had looked at with such interest, as if they were acquaintances of his, in the days when he was only a poor surveying-clerk. But these were merely the first steps in his art as a speculator. No great cleverness was needed to run out leases, conspire with tenants, and rob the State and individuals; nor did he think the game worth the candle. This was why he soon used his genius for transactions of a more complicated nature.

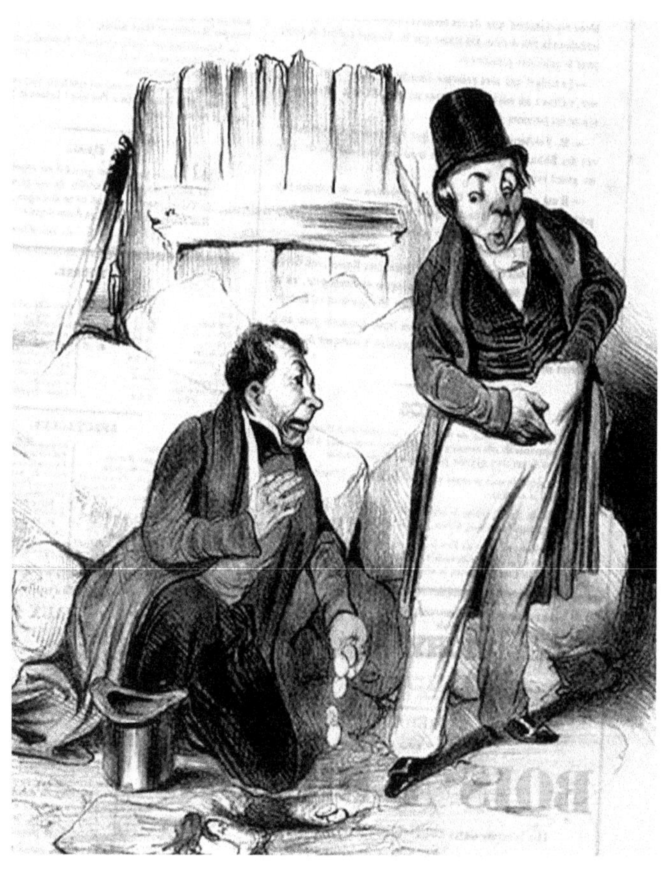

The buried pot trick.

You see, says the rogue to the country cousin, when one goes into these houses here, it is necessary to go without money. Accordingly he deposits his own money and that of the simpleton in a hiding place. Hardly have they left together, an associate comes to take the hidden treasure. This theft is called the buried pot trick.

Honoré Daumier, *Le Charivari,* 18 December1836

Saccard first invented the trick of making secret purchases of house property on the City's account. A decision of the Council of State had placed the City in a difficult position. It had acquired by private contract a large number of houses, in the hope of running out the leases and turning the tenants out without compensation. But these purchases were pronounced to be genuine acts of expropriation, and the City had to pay. It was then that Saccard offered to lend his name to the City: he bought houses, ran out the leases, and for a consideration handed over the property at a fixed date. He even began to play a double game: he acted as buyer both for the City and for the Prefect. Whenever the deal was irresistibly tempting, he stuck to the house himself. The State paid. In return for his assistance he received building concessions for bits of streets, for open spaces, which he disposed of before the new boulevard was even begun. It was a tremendous gamble: the new neighbourhoods were speculated in as one speculates in stocks and shares. Certain ladies were involved, beautiful women, intimately connected with some of the prominent officials; one of them, whose white teeth are world-famous, has eaten up whole streets on more than one occasion. Saccard was insatiable, he felt his greed grow at the sight of the flood of gold that glided through his fingers. It seemed to him as if a sea of twenty-franc pieces stretched out around him, swelling from a lake to an ocean, filling the vast horizon with a strange sound of waves, a metallic music that tickled his heart; and he grew bolder, plunging deeper every day, diving and coming up again, now on his back, now on his belly, swimming through this great expanse in fair weather and foul, and relying on his strength and skill to prevent him from ever sinking to the bottom.

Paris was at that time disappearing in a cloud of plaster-dust.

Émile Zola, *The Kill*

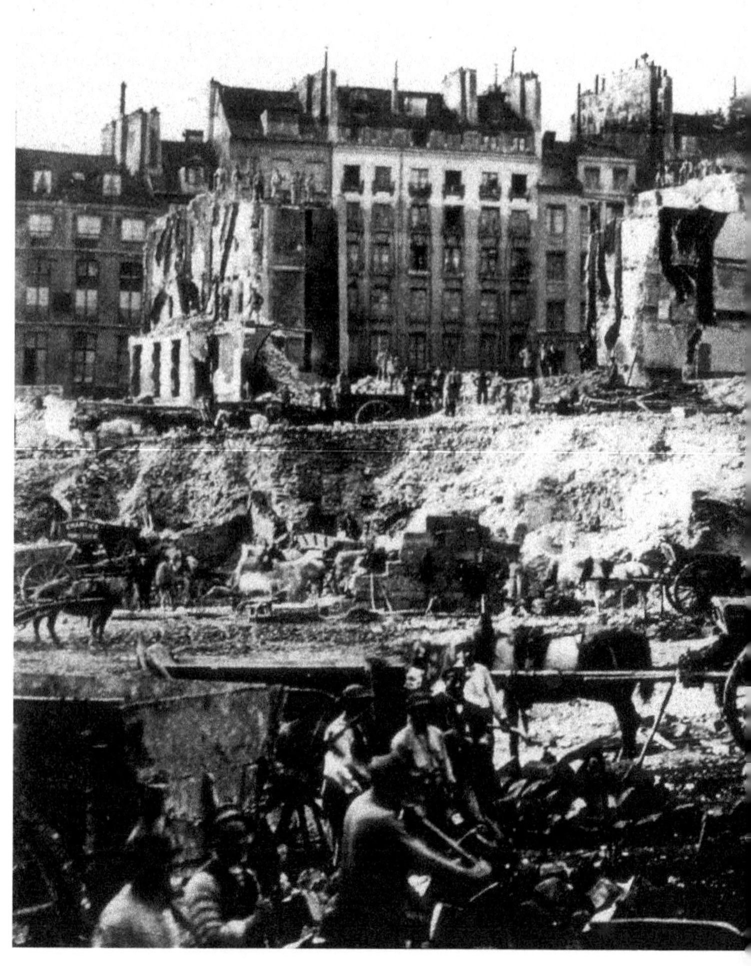

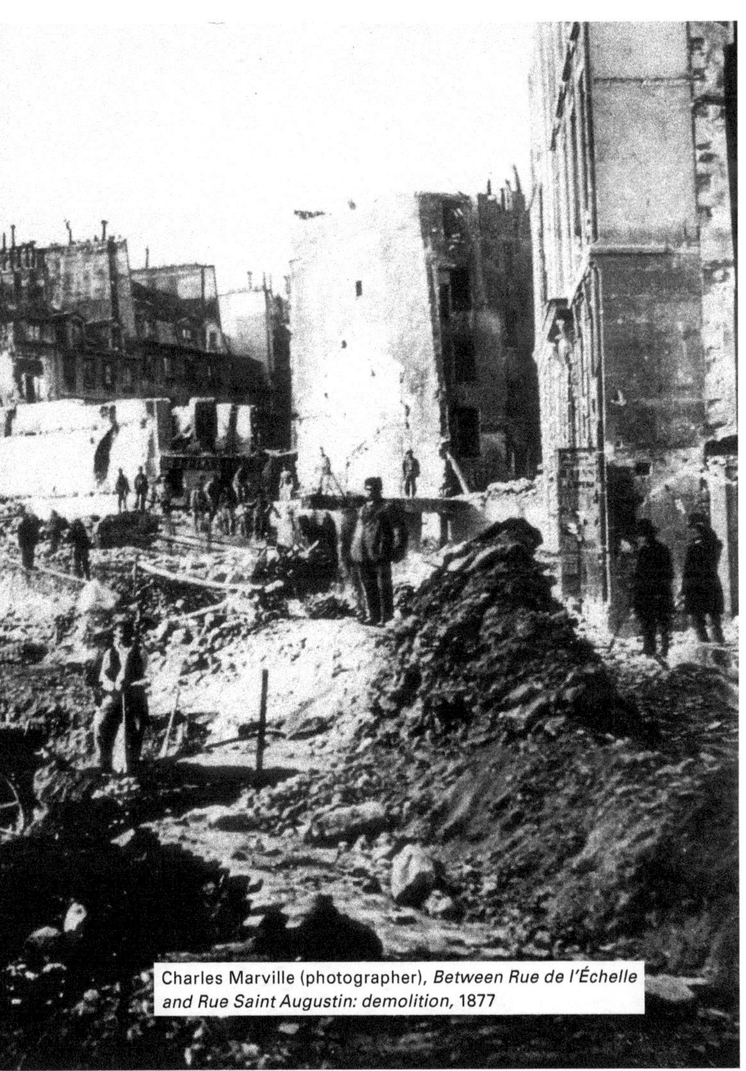

Charles Marville (photographer), *Between Rue de l'Échelle and Rue Saint Augustin: demolition,* 1877

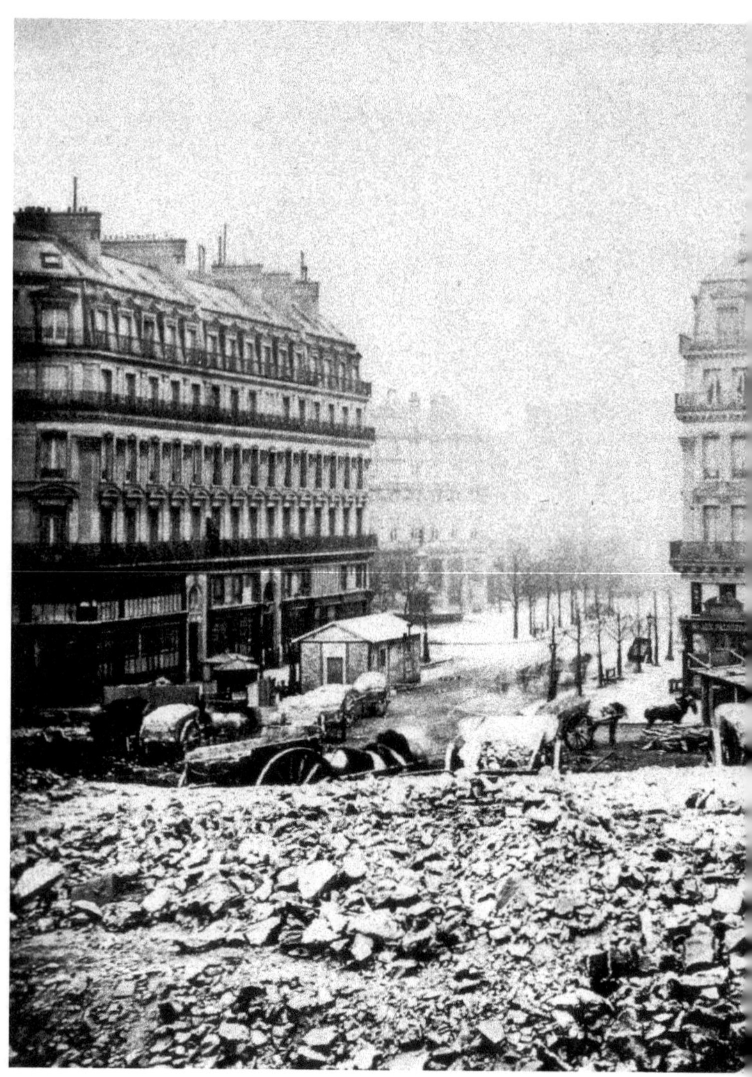

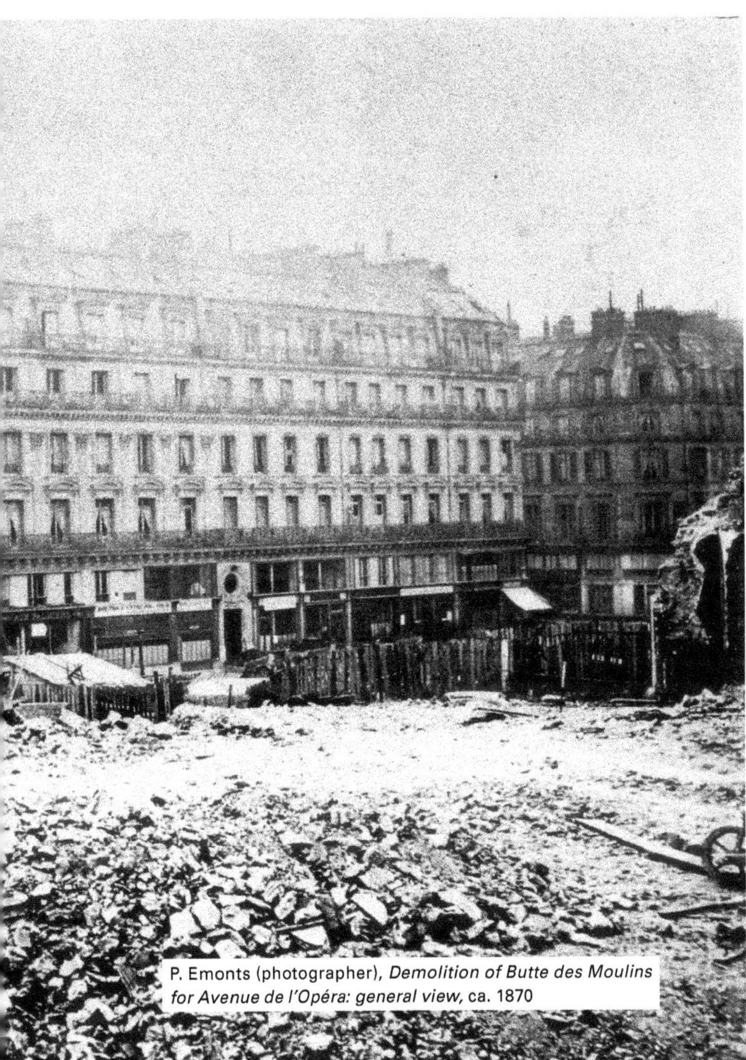

P. Emonts (photographer), *Demolition of Butte des Moulins for Avenue de l'Opéra: general view,* ca. 1870

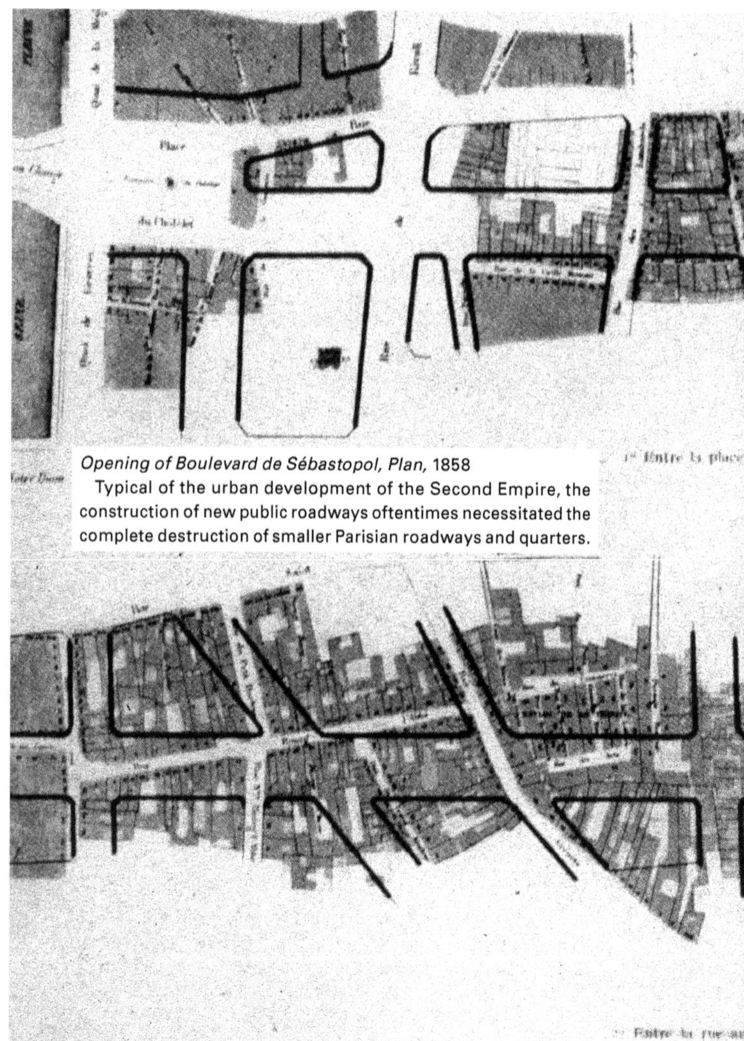

Opening of Boulevard de Sébastopol, Plan, 1858
Typical of the urban development of the Second Empire, the construction of new public roadways oftentimes necessitated the complete destruction of smaller Parisian roadways and quarters.

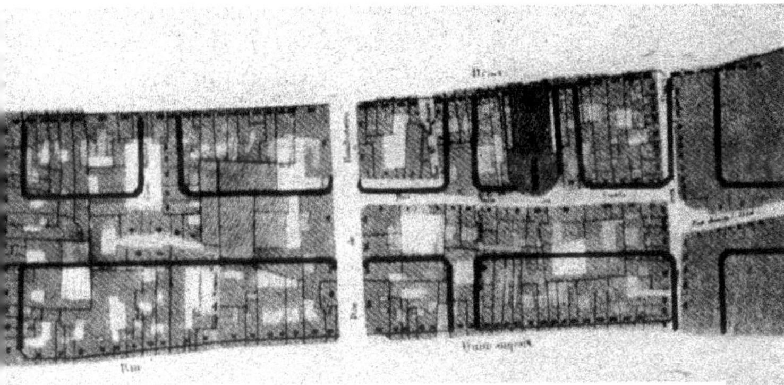

As predicted by Haussmann, the Boulevard de Sébastopol, designed to run parallel with the rues Saint-Martin and Saint-Denis, would not only prove to be efficient in decreasing travel congestion, but also in helping to contain potential riots in the densely populated Parisian neighborhoods.

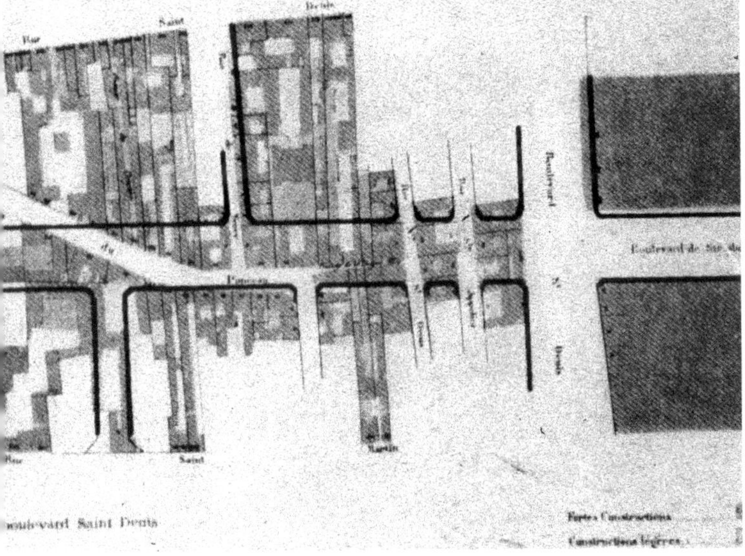

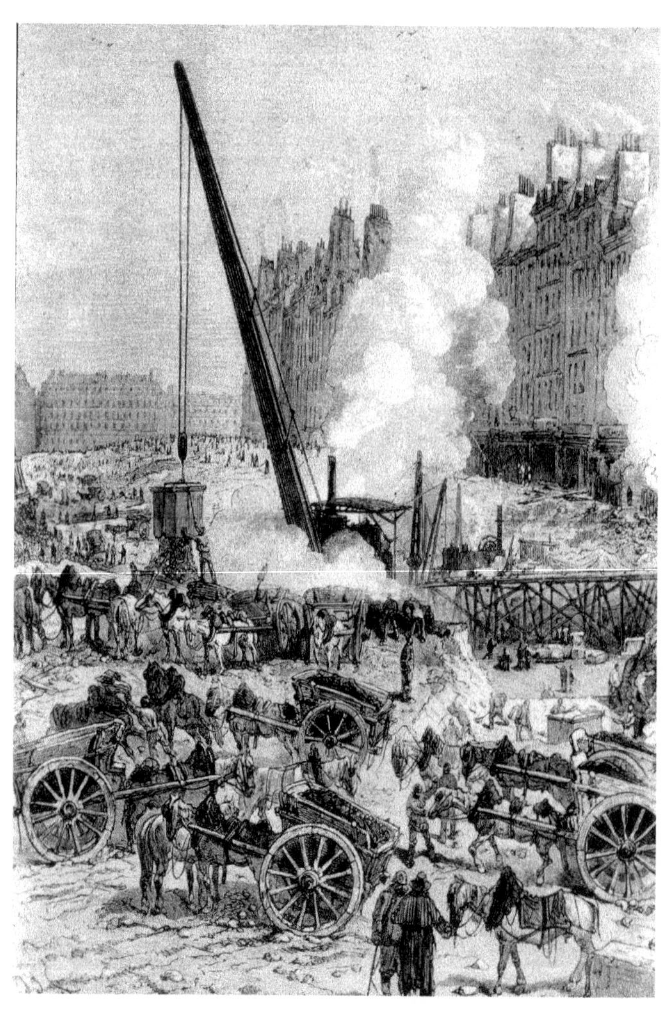

Jules Descartes Férat, *Demolition for Avenue de l'Opéra: between rue de l'Échelle and rue Saint Roch*

Before long, turning over money by the shovelful, he had eight houses on the new boulevards. He had four that were completely finished: two in the Rue de Marignan, and two on the Boulevard Haussmann; the four others, situated on the Boulevard Malesherbes, remained in progress, and one of them, in fact, a vast enclosure of planks from which a mansion was to arise, had got no further than the flooring of the first storey. At this period his affairs became so complicated, he had his fingers in so many pies, that he slept barely three hours a night and read his correspondence in his carriage. The marvellous thing was that his coffers seemed inexhaustible. He held shares in every company, built houses with a sort of mania, turned to every trade, and threatened to inundate Paris like a rising tide; and yet he was never seen to realize a genuine clear profit, to pocket a big sum of gold shining in the sun. This flood of gold with no known source, which seemed to flow from his office in endless waves, astonished the onlookers and made him, at one moment, a prominent public figure to whom the newspapers ascribed all the witticisms that came out of the Bourse.

With such a husband Renée could hardly be said to be married at all. She would hardly see him for weeks. For the rest he was perfect; his cash-box was always open. She liked him as she would have liked an obliging banker. When she visited the Hôtel Béraud, she praised him to the skies to her father, whose cold austerity remained quite unaffected by his son-in-law's good fortune. Her contempt had disappeared: this man seemed so convinced that life is a mere business, he was so obviously born to make money with whatever fell into his hands—women, children, paving-stones, sacks of plaster, consciences—that she could no longer reproach him for their marriage-bargain. Since that bargain he regarded her rather like one of the fine houses he owned and which would, he hoped, yield a large profit. He liked to see her well-dressed, flamboyant, attracting the attention of Tout Paris. It consolidated his position, doubled the probable size of his fortune. He seemed young, handsome, in love, and scatter-brained because of his wife. She was his partner, his unconscious accomplice. A new pair of horses, a two-thousand-crown dress, the indulgence of some lover facilitated and often ensured the success of his most successful transactions. He often pretended to be tired out and sent her to a minister, to some functionary or other, to solicit an authorization or receive a reply. He would say 'Be good!' in a tone all his own, at once bantering and coaxing; and when she returned, having succeeded, he would rub his hands, repeating his famous 'I hope you were good!' Renée would laugh. He was too busy to desire a Madame Michelin. But he loved crude jokes and risqué stories. For the rest, had Renée not 'been good', he would have experienced only the disappointment of having really paid for the minister's or the functionary's indulgence. To dupe people, to give them less than their money's-worth, was his delight. He often said: 'If I were a woman, I might sell myself, but I'd never deliver the goods: that's stupid!'

Émile Zola, *The Kill*

Meanwhile the Saccards' fortune seemed to be at its height. It blazed in the heart of Paris like a huge bonfire. This was the time when the rush for spoils filled a corner of the forest with the yelping of hounds, the cracking of whips, the flaring of torches. The appetites let loose were satisfied at last, shamelessly, amid the sound of crumbling neighbourhoods and fortunes made in six months. The city had become an orgy of gold and women. Vice, coming from on high, flowed through the gutters, spread out over the ornamental waters, shot up in the fountains of the public gardens, and fell on the roofs as fine rain. At night, when people crossed the bridges, it seemed as if the Seine drew along with it, through the sleeping city, all the refuse of the streets, crumbs fallen from tables, bows of lace left on couches, false hair forgotten in cabs, banknotes that had slipped out of bodices, everything thrown out of the window by the brutality of desire and the immediate satisfaction of appetites. Then, amid the troubled sleep of Paris, and even more clearly than during its feverish quest in broad daylight, one felt a growing sense of madness, the voluptuous nightmare of a city obsessed with gold and flesh.

Émile Zola, *The Kill*

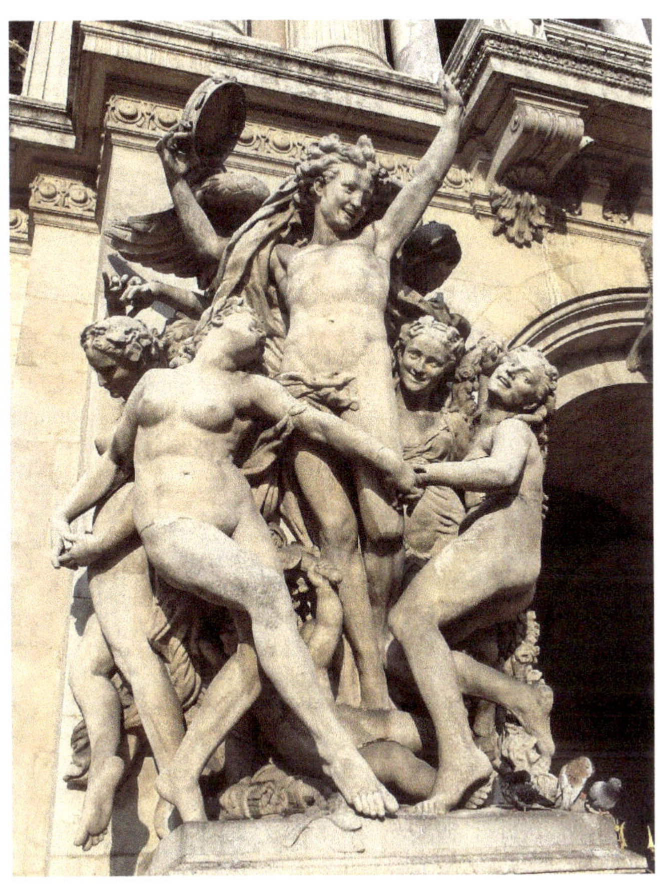

Jean-Baptiste Carpeaux, *The Dance,* 1869

"... take Carpeaux' celebrated group *The Dance* on the facade of the Paris Opera House. Here the idea of the excitement and abandon of the dance is splendidly conveyed in figures which represent no special period or country, but are the abstract and poetic expression of human feeling and action."

"A Colonial Discussion on Art," *The Builder,* 19 September 1885

He had a way of enumerating his riches that bewildered his listeners and prevented them from seeing the truth. His Provençal accent grew more pronounced: with his short phrases and nervous gestures he let off fireworks in which millions shot up like rockets and ended by dazzling the most incredulous. These frenetic performances were mainly responsible for his reputation as a lucky speculator. In truth, no one knew whether he had any solid capital assets. His various partners, who were necessarily acquainted with his position as regards themselves, explained his colossal fortune by believing in his absolute luck in other speculations, those in which they had no share. He spent money madly; the flow from his cash-box continued, though the sources of that stream of gold had not yet been discovered. It was pure folly, a frenzy of money, handfuls of louis flung out of the windows, the safe emptied every evening to its last sou, filling up again during the night, no one knew how, and never supplying such large sums as when Saccard pretended to have lost the keys.

Émile Zola, *The Kill*

He set foot barely once a month in Renée's bedroom, and always concerning some delicate question of money.

Émile Zola, *The Kill*

The truth was that Renée's dowry had been exhausted long ago; it had become a fictitious asset in Saccard's safe. Although he paid out interest on it at the rate of two or three hundred per cent or more, he could not have produced the least security or found the smallest solid particle of the original capital. As he half confessed, moreover, the five hundred thousand francs of the Sologne property had been used to pay a first instalment on the house and the furniture, which together cost nearly two million. He still owed a million to the upholsterer and the builders.

'I don't want to make any claims on you,' Renée said at last. 'I know I'm very much in your debt.'

'Oh, my dear,' he cried, taking his wife's hand, without letting go of the tongs, 'what a dreadful thing to say! Listen, the long and the

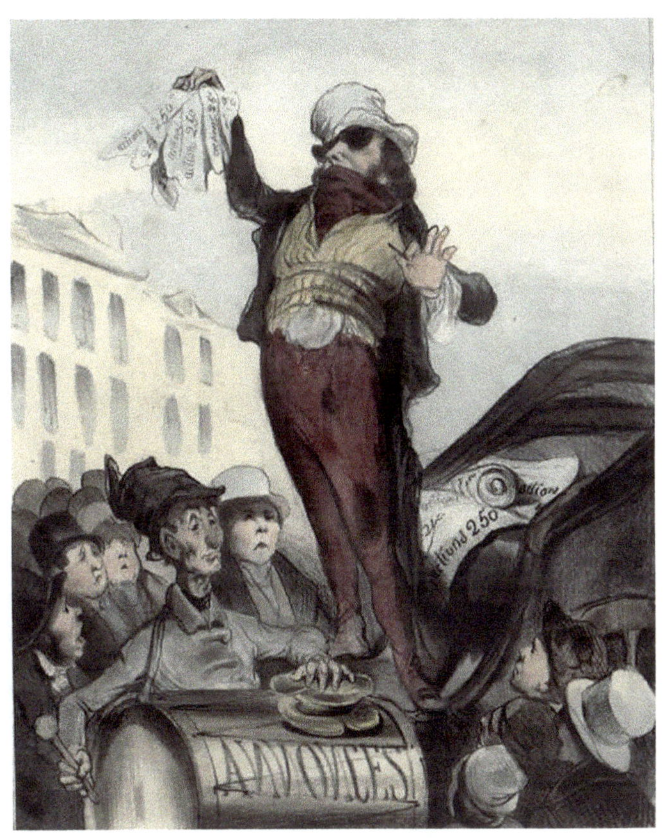

Ladies and gentlemen!

Silver mines, gold mines, diamond mines are only thin gruel and stale rolls in comparison with coal ... But even so, (you're going to say), you're selling your shares for a million?... I'm not selling my shares, gentlemen, I'm giving them away for 200 miserable francs, I'm giving two for every one, I'm giving away a needle, an ear-pick, a bodkin, and what's more, I give you my blessing into the bargain. Bring out the big drum!

Honoré Daumier, *Le Charivari,* 7 October 1836

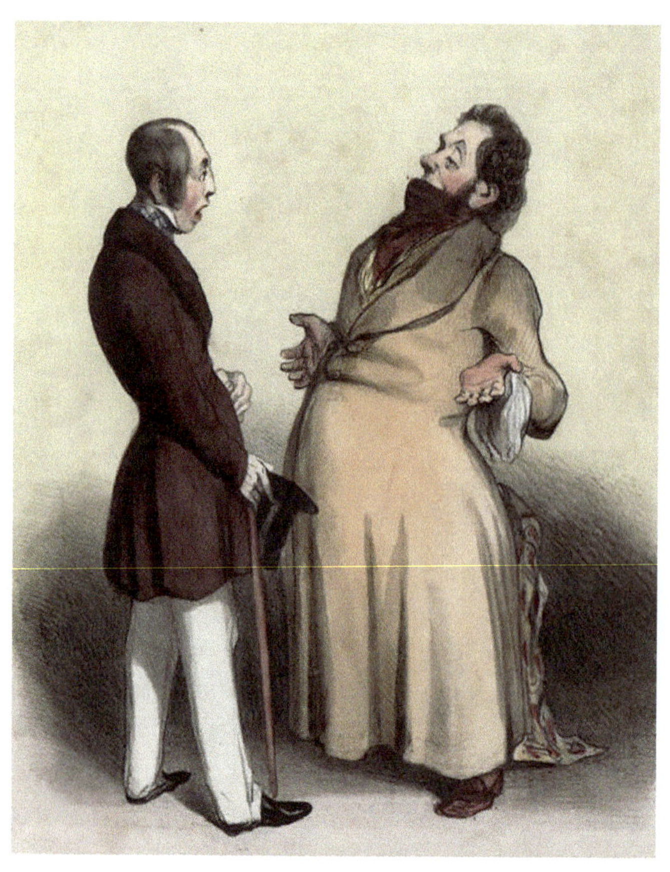

Robert Macaire, discount broker.

Here are my conditions. You make me out a bill of exchange for 40'000 Fr. and I'll give you 25 Fr. in cash, 3'000 Fr. worth of white mustard and articulated clogs, 3'000 Fr. worth of chips, a carriage wheel, two cows, four shares in Physionotype and a quintal of useful facts ... I don't have any other assets in hand, but these are worth their weight in gold.

Honoré Daumier, *Le Charivari,* 27 September 1836

short of it is that I have had some bad luck at the Bourse, Toutin-Laroche has got himself into a mess, and Mignon and Charrier are a pair of crooks. That's why I can't pay your bill. You will forgive me, won't you?'

He seemed genuinely upset. He dug the tongs in among the logs and made the sparks fly up like fireworks. Renée remembered how restless he had been recently. But she was unable to realize the amazing truth. Saccard had reached the point of having to perform a daily miracle. He lived like a king in a house that cost two million, but there were mornings when he had not a thousand francs in his safe. He did not seem to spend any less. He lived on debt among an army of creditors who swallowed up each day the scandalous profits he made from his transactions. In the meantime companies crumbled beneath his feet, new and deeper holes yawned before him, over which he had to leap, unable to fill them up. He thus trod over a minefield, living in a constant state of crisis, settling bills of fifty thousand francs but leaving his coachman's wages unpaid, marching on with ever-more regal assurance, emptying over Paris with increasing frenzy his empty cash-box, from which the golden stream with the fabulous source never stopped flowing.

The world of speculation was going through a difficult period. Saccard was a worthy offspring of the Hôtel de Ville. He had experienced the rapid transformations, the frenzied pursuit of pleasure, the blindness to expense that had convulsed Paris. Now, like the City, he found himself faced with a huge deficit which he had secretly to make good, for he would not hear of prudence, of economy, of a peaceful and respectable existence. He preferred to keep up the useless luxury and real penury of the new boulevards, which had provided him with his colossal fortune which came into being every morning only to be swallowed up by nightfall. Moving from one adventure to the next, he now possessed only the gilded façade of missing capital. In this period of utter madness, Paris itself did not risk its future with greater rashness or hurry more directly towards every folly and every trick of finance.

Émile Zola, *The Kill*

'We speculators, my dear, are like pretty women, we have our little tricks ...'

Émile Zola, *The Kill*

Her soft voice came out of the darkness.

'Money troubles again?' she asked, as if she had said troubles of the heart, in a voice full of gentleness and compassion.

Renée lowered her eyes and nodded.

'Ah! if my brothers listened to me, we would all be rich. But they just shrug when I mention that debt of three thousand million francs. I'm still hoping, nevertheless. For the last ten years I've wanted to go across to England. I'm so busy, though! But I decided to write to London, and I'm waiting for a reply.'

As the younger woman smiled, she went on:

'I know you think it's all nonsense. But you'd be very pleased if one of these days I gave you a million francs. The story is very simple: there was a Parisian banker who lent the money to the king of England, and as the banker died without direct heirs, the State is entitled to claim the debt back with compound interest. I've worked it out, it comes to over two thousand, nine hundred and forty-three million, two hundred and ten thousand francs. Don't worry, it will come, it will come.'

'In the meantime,' said Renée, with a touch of irony, 'I wish you would get someone to lend me a hundred thousand francs. Then I could pay my dressmaker, who is always pestering me.'

'A hundred thousand francs can be found,' calmly replied Madame Sidonie. 'It's just a question of what you'll give in exchange.'

Émile Zola, *The Kill*

He contented himself with preparing the dénouement by continuing to give her no money except through Larsonneau. When he had a few thousand francs to spare, and she complained of her poverty, he brought them to her, saying that Larsonneau's people required a promissory note for twice as much. This farce amused him greatly, the story of the promissory notes delighting him because of the air of romance they imparted to the affair. Even during the period

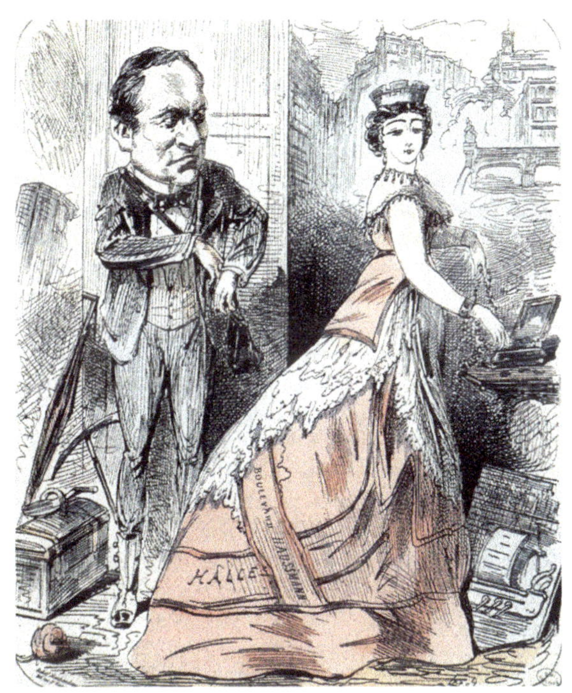

M. Haussmann et Mlle Lutèce.

Paris-Comique, 1870

Originally appearing on the cover of the January 15th, 1870 issue of "Paris-Comique", this anonymous engraving was printed with the following caption: "Est-il possible qu'après vous avoir tant aimée, qu'après vous avoir coverte de perles et de diamants, et fait de vous, jadis si laide, la plus belle ... fille de la terre, vous me disiez ... zut? Ingrate!!"

It was not unusual for 19th century artists to personify Paris as female. This artist presents Haussmann's Paris as his dependent yet ungrateful mistress. Haussmann, as well as many of his associates, felt unappreciated and wronged by the constant criticism they faced regarding their urban developmental projects in Paris.

Brown University Library, *Paris: Capital of the 19th Century*

of his biggest profits he had served out his wife's income in a very irregular fashion, giving her princely presents, throwing her handfuls of banknotes, and then for weeks leaving her just a paltry amount. Now that he found himself in dire straits, he spoke of the household expenses, treating her like a creditor to whom one is unwilling to confess one's ruin, gaining time by making excuses. She barely listened to him; she signed anything, sorry that she was not able to sign more.

Already, however, he held two hundred thousand francs' worth of her promissory notes, which had cost him barely one hundred and ten thousand francs. After having these notes endorsed by Larsonneau, to whom they were made out, he put them prudently into circulation, intending to use them as decisive weapons later on. He would never have been able to hold out to the end of that terrible winter, lending money to his wife like a usurer and keeping up his domestic expenses, had it not been for the sale of his building-plots on the Boulevard Malesherbes, which Mignon and Charrier bought from him in cash, deducting a huge discount.

For Renée this same winter was a time of joy. She suffered only from a lack of ready money.

Émile Zola, *The Kill*

Monsieur Hupel de la Noue had come up to the group standing behind the Baron's armchair, when the piano struck up a triumphal march. A loud burst of harmony, produced by masterful strokes on the keyboard, introduced a full melody in which a metallic clang resounded at intervals. As each phrase was finished, it was repeated in a higher key that accentuated the rhythm. It was at once fierce and joyous.

'You'll see,' murmured Monsieur Hupel de la Noue, 'that I have perhaps carried poetic licence too far, but I think my boldness has worked. Echo, seeing that Venus has no power over Narcissus, takes him to Plutus, the god of wealth and precious metals. After the temptation of the flesh, the temptation of riches.'

'That's very classical,' replied Monsieur Toutin-Laroche, with an amiable smile. 'You know your period, Monsieur le Préfet.'

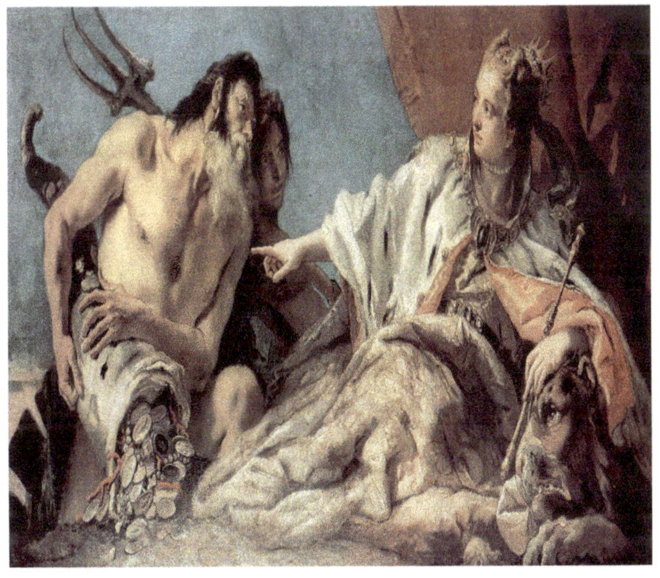

Giovanni Battista Tiepolo, *Neptune Offering Gifts to Venice,* 1750

Venice is shown as an imperious mistress of the seas to whom the god pours out his cornucopia of gold. And this just at the time when the Venetian Empire in the Eastern Mediterranean had been finally absorbed by the Turks. By the Treaty of Passarowitz of 1718, signed two years before the painting was completed, Venice ceased to be a European Power and abdicated her political role in Europe. This painting, too, we must surely conclude, like Tiepolo's *Apotheosis of Spain,* is really a dream about a golden past.

Bernard Smith, *Tiepolo*

The curtains parted, the piano played more loudly. The spectacle was dazzling. The electric light fell on a scene of fiery splendour in which the spectators at first saw nothing but a brazier, in which precious stones and ingots of gold seemed to be melting. A new grotto revealed itself; but this was not the cool retreat of Venus, lapped by waters eddying on fine sand bestrewn with pearls, but one situated seemingly in the centre of the earth, in a fiery nether region, a fissure of the hell of antiquity, a crevice in a mine of molten metals inhabited by Plutus. The silk simulating rock showed broad threads of metal, layers that looked like the veins of a primeval world, loaded with incalculable riches and the eternal life of the earth. On the ground, thanks to a bold anachronism of Monsieur Hupel de la Noue's, lay a great pile of twenty-franc pieces.

On top of this pile of gold sat Madame de Guende as Plutus, a female Plutus with generously displayed breasts set in the great stripes of her dress, which represented all the metals. Around the god, erect, reclining, grouped in clusters, or blooming apart, were posed the fairy-like flora of the grotto, into which the caliphs of the Arabian Nights seemed to have emptied their treasures: Madame Haffner as Gold, with a stiff, resplendent skirt like a bishop's cape; Madame d'Espanet as Silver, gleaming like moonlight; Madame de Lauwerens in bright blue, as a Sapphire, and by her side little Madame Daste, a smiling Turquoise in the softest blue; then there was an Emerald, Madame de Meinhold; a Topaz, Madame Teissière; and lower down, the Comtesse Vanska, lending her dark ardour to a Coral, recumbent, with raised arms loaded with rosy pendants, like a monstrous, seductive polyp displaying a woman's flesh amidst the yawning, pink pearliness of its shell. All of these ladies wore necklaces, bracelets, sets of jewels formed of the precious stones they impersonated. Especially noticeable were the jewels worn by Mesdames d'Espanet and Haffner, made up entirely of small gold and silver coins fresh from the mint. In the foreground the story remained unchanged: Echo was still tempting Narcissus, who continued to reject her overtures. The spectators' eyes were getting used to this yawning cavity opening onto the flaming bowels of the earth, onto this pile of gold upon which were strewn the riches of a world.

This second tableau was even more successful than the first. It seemed particularly ingenious. The audacity of the twenty-franc pieces, this stream of money from a modern safe that had fallen into a corner of Greek mythology, captured the imagination of the ladies and financiers present. The words, 'So much gold! So much money!' flitted round, with smiles, with long tremors of satisfaction; and each of these ladies and gentlemen dreamt of owning all this money themselves, coffered in their cellars.

'England has paid up; there are your millions,' Louise whispered maliciously in Madame Sidonie's ear.

Madame Michelin, her mouth slightly open with desire, threw back her almah's veil and fondled the gold with glittering eyes, while the group of serious-looking gentlemen went into transports of delight. Monsieur Toutin-Laroche, beaming, whispered a few words in the ear of the Baron, whose face was becoming covered with yellow blotches; while Mignon and Charrier, less discreet, crudely exclaimed:

'Damn it! There's enough there to demolish the whole of Paris and rebuild it.'

This remark seemed quite profound to Saccard, who was beginning to suspect that Mignon and Charrier just made fun of people under the pretence of idiocy. When the curtains fell once more, and the piano finished its triumphal march with a tumult of notes thrown pell-mell, like a last shovelful of crown pieces, there was a burst of applause ...

Émile Zola, *The Kill*

She looked down, and when she saw herself in her tights, and in her light gauze blouse, she gazed at herself with lowered eyes and sudden blushes. Who had stripped her naked? What was she doing there, bare-breasted, like a prostitute displaying herself almost to the waist? She no longer knew. She looked at her thighs, rounded out by the tights; at her hips, whose supple outlines she could see under the gauze; at her breasts, barely covered. She was ashamed of herself, and contempt for her body filled her with mute anger at those who had left her like this, with mere bangles of gold at her wrists and ankles to cover her skin ...

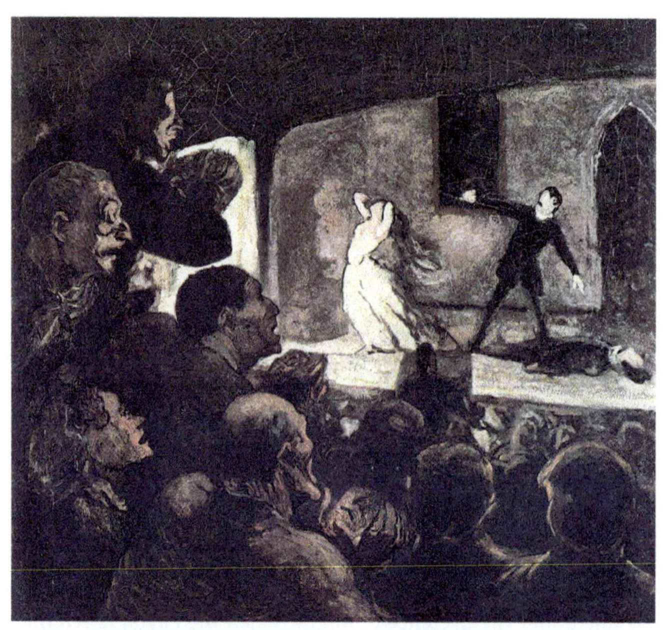

Honoré Daumier, *The Drama,* 1860

Some Observations About Theatric Life During This Period

The financial aspects between artists and the director of the theater can at best be described as highly unusual. On June 28, 1843 the *Charivari* published the following comments: "What a bizarre world, what contrasts, what a mix up of existences of these pariahs of civilization. What a life of nomads, and what daily misery ... Daumier shows us all this with his drawing pencil ..." As one can see in these prints, Daumier is frequently touched by the poverty, ridicule and dependence of the artist ... quite often a Hamlet or Agamemnon will go to bed with just a piece of bread for dinner. As the story goes, the director of a theatre in that period paid his leading actor very well, while the understudy received no salary at all or even had to pay for the privilege of acting. Most of the actors had a very insecure existence. Pretty young ladies who were using the stage as a stepping-stone for a position in society as a matter of rule had to pay for the chance to appear on stage.

Dieter Noack and Lilian Noack, *The Daumier Register*

Her life unfurled before her. She recalled her growing alarm, the cacophony of gold and flesh rising within her, at first coming up to her knees, then to her belly, then to her lips; and now she felt it submerging her, pounding on her skull. It was like a poisonous sap: it had weakened her limbs, grafted growths of shameful affection on her heart, made sickly, bestial caprices sprout in her brain. This sap had soaked into her feet on the rug of her barouche, on other carpets too, on all the silk and velvet on which she had been walking since her marriage. The footsteps of others must have left behind those poisonous seeds, which were now germinating in her blood and circulating in her veins ...

Who then, had stripped her naked?

In the dim blue reflection of the glass she imagined she saw the figures of Saccard and Maxime rise up. Saccard, swarthy, grinning, iron-hued, with his cruel laugh and skinny legs. The strength of the man's will! For ten years she had seen him at the forge amid the sparks of red-hot metal, his flesh scorched, breathless, pounding away, lifting hammers twenty times too heavy for his arms, at the risk of crushing himself. She understood him now; he seemed to have grown taller through his superhuman efforts, his stupendous roguery, his obsession with money. She remembered how he leapt over obstacles, rolling in the mud, not bothering to wipe himself down, so that he could reach his goal more quickly, not even stopping to enjoy himself on the way, chewing on his twenty-franc pieces as he ran. Then Maxime's pretty, fair-haired head appeared behind his father's shoulder: he had his prostitute's smile, his vacant, lascivious eyes, which were never lowered, his centre parting, which showed the whiteness of his skull. He laughed at Saccard, upon whom he looked down for taking so much trouble to make the money which he, Maxime, spent with such adorable ease. He was like a kept woman. His soft, slender hands bore witness to his vices. His smooth body had the languid attitude of satiated desire. In all his soft, feeble person, through which vice coursed gently like warm water, there shone not even a gleam of the curiosity of sin. He was a passive agent. Renée, as she looked at these two apparitions emerging from the faint shadows of the mirror, stepped back, saw that Saccard had used her like a stake, like an investment, and that Maxime had happened to be there to pick up the louis fallen from the gambler's pocket. She was an asset in her husband's portfolio; he urged her to buy gowns for an evening, to take lovers for a season; he wrought her in the flames of his forge, using her as a precious metal with which to gild the iron of his hands. So, little by little, the father had driven her to such a pitch of madness and abandonment as to desire the kisses of the son. If Maxime was the impoverished blood of Saccard, she felt that she was the product, the maggot-eaten fruit of the two men, the pit of infamy they had dug between them, and into which they now both rolled.

She knew now. It was they who had stripped her naked. Saccard had unhooked her bodice, and Maxime had pulled down her skirt. Then, between them, they had torn off her shift. Now she stood there without a rag, with gold bracelets, like a slave.

Émile Zola, *The Kill*

'We've finished,' said the latter, returning to the garden. 'If you will allow me, Messieurs, I'll draw up the report.'

The manufacturer of surgical instruments did not even hear. He was deep in the Regency.

'What strange times, all the same!' he murmured. Then they found a cab in the Rue de Charonne, and drove off, splashed up to their knees, but as satisfied with their walk as if they had had a day in the country. In the cab the conversation changed, they talked politics, they said that the Emperor was doing great things. No one had ever seen the like of what they had just seen. That great, long, straight street would be splendid when the houses were built.

Saccard drew up the report, and the Authority granted three million francs. The speculator was in dire straits, he could not have waited another month. This money saved him from ruin and even from the dock. He paid five hundred thousand francs towards the million he owed his upholsterer and his builder for the house in the Parc Monceau. He stopped up other holes, launched new companies, deafened Paris with the sound of the real crown pieces he shovelled out onto the shelves of his iron safe. The golden stream had a source

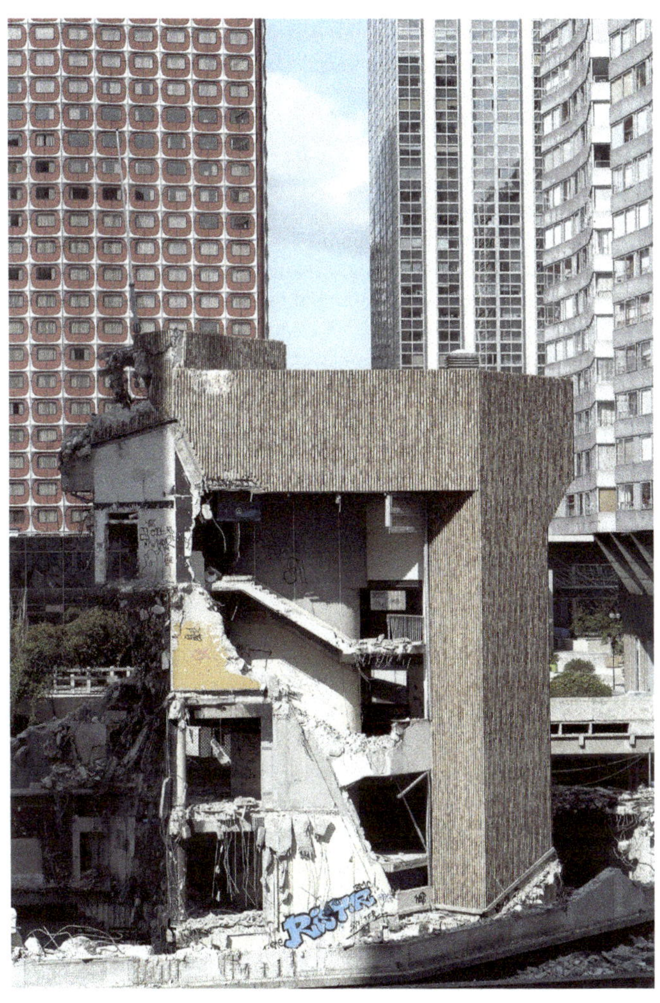

Ted Bassman (photographer), *Demolition du Centre Commercial Beaugrenelle à Paris,* 2009

at last. But it was not yet a solid, established fortune, flowing with an even, continuous current. Saccard, saved from a crisis, thought himself a beggar with the crumbs from his three million, and said frankly that he was still too poor, that he could not stop; and soon the ground appeared once more to be giving way under his feet.

Larsonneau had conducted himself so admirably in the Charonne affair that Saccard, after a brief hesitation, had the honesty to give him his ten per cent and his bonus of thirty thousand francs. The expropriation agent immediately set up a banking house. When his accomplice peevishly accused him of being richer than himself, the yellow-gloved dandy replied with a laugh:

'You see, master, you're very clever at making the five-franc pieces rain down, but you don't know how to pick them up.'

Madame Sidonie took advantage of her brother's stroke of luck to borrow ten thousand francs from him, and used them to spend two months in London. She returned without a sou. It was never known where the ten thousand francs had gone.

'Good gracious!' she replied, when they asked her about it, 'it all costs money. I ransacked all the libraries. I had three secretaries helping me.'

When she was asked if she had at last some positive information about the three thousand million, she smiled mysteriously, and muttered:

'You're a lot of unbelievers ... I've discovered nothing, but it makes no difference. You'll see one of these days.'

Émile Zola, *The Kill*

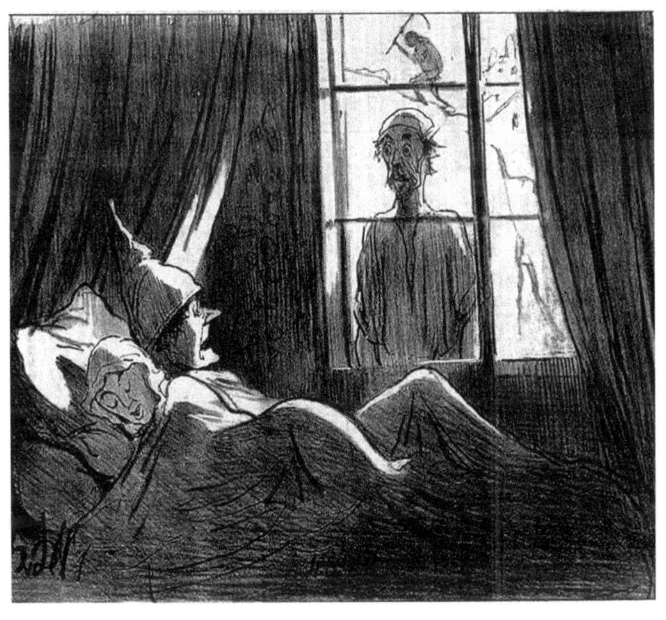

Come on citizen, wake up! It's your turn to be demolished now.

Honoré Daumier, *Le Charivari,* 27 December 1852

NOTES

2–J. Chein & Co., *Vintage Tin World Globe Bank,* Seller: larry7511 (99.3% Positive feedback), *ebay,* 28 November 2013, www.ebay.com. **5**–WritingResource.info,"Capital Letters (Printable Handout)," *WritingResource.info,* 2011, http://www.writingresource.info/capitals.html. **9**–Émile Zola, *The Kill,* 1872, translated by Brian Nelson, London, Oxford University Press, 2004, 61. **10**–Lewis Lapham, "Ignorance of Things Past: Who Wins and Who Loses When We Forget American History," *Harper's Magazine,* May 2012, 30-31. **10**–Émile Zola, *The Kill,* 27-8. **10**–Lewis Lapham, "Ignorance of Things Past," 30-31. **11**–Dieter Noack and Lilian Noack, *The Daumier Register Digital Work Catalogue,* http://www.daumier-register.org. **12**–Émile Zola, *The Kill,* 25. **12**–Lewis Lapham, "Ignorance of Things Past," 30-31. **13**–Dieter Noack and Lilian Noack, *The Daumier Register.* **14**–Émile Zola, *The Kill,* 26-27. **15**–Brown University Library, "Paris: Capital of the 19th Century," *Brown University Library Center for Digital Scholarship,* http://library.brown.edu/cds/paris. **16**–Ibid. **17**–Lewis Lapham, "Ignorance of Things Past," 30-31. **17**–Émile Zola, *The Kill,* 25-26. **18**–Brown University Library, "Paris: Capital of the 19th Century." **18**–Philip E. Bishop, *Adventures in the Human Spirit,* Upper Saddle River, NJ, Prentice Hall, 2011, 356-57. **19**–Émile Zola, *The Kill,* 48-50. **20**–Dieter Noack and Lilian Noack, *The Daumier Register.* **22**–Brown University Library, "Paris: Capital of the 19th Century." **23**–Sam Lipsyte, "The Republic of Empathy," *The New Yorker,* June 4 & 11, 2012, 62. **24**–n+1 Magazine. "Death By Degrees," *n+1 Magazine,* 19 June 2012, http://nplusonemag.com/death-by-degrees. **25**–Dieter Noack and Lilian Noack, *The Daumier Register.* **26**–Sam Lipsyte, "The Republic of Empathy," 62. **26**–n+1 Magazine, "Death By Degrees." **27**–Dieter Noack and Lilian Noack, *The Daumier Register.* **28**–Émile Zola, *The Kill,* 62. **28**–Sam Lipsyte, "The Republic of Empathy," 62. **28**–Émile Zola, *The Kill,* 63-64. **28**–Ibid., 67. **29**–Brown University Library, "Paris: Capital of the 19th Century." **30**–Ibid. **31**–Émile Zola, *The Kill,* 67-68. **33**–Ibid., 93-94. **34**–Dieter Noack and Lilian Noack, *The Daumier Register.* **36**–Brown University Library, "Paris: Capital of the 19th Century." **38**–Ibid. **40**–Ibid. **42**–Ibid. **43**–Émile Zola, *The Kill,* 98-99. **44**–Ibid., 112. **45**–Khan Academy, "Carpeaux's Dance," *Smart History,* http://smarthistory.khanacademy.org/carpeauxs-dance.html. **46**–Émile Zola, *The Kill,* 113. **46**–Ibid., 135. **46**–Ibid., 137-38. **47**–Dieter Noack and Lilian Noack, *The Daumier Register.* **48**–Ibid. **50**–Émile Zola, *The Kill,* 139-40. **50**–Ibid., 145-46. **50**–Ibid., 164. **51**–Brown University Library, "Paris: Capital of the 19th Century." **52**–Émile Zola, *The Kill,* 216-18. **53**–Kalina, "Cybele, Isis, Serapis, Fortuna, Hades, Horn of Plenty, Wheel of Fortune, Pine Cone," *Creativity and Healing,* http://creativityandhealing-kalina.blogspot.ca/2011/12/i-have-seen-from-darkness-to-light.html. **55**–Émile Zola, *The Kill,* 240-41. **56**–Dieter Noack and Lilian Noack, *The Daumier Register.* **58**–Émile Zola, *The Kill,* 252-3. **59**–Ted Bassman, *Demolition Du Centre Commercial Beaugrenelle À Paris,* 2009, www.flickr.com/photos/tedbassman/5253651651. **61**–Dieter Noack and Lilian Noack, *The Daumier Register.* **65**–*Wikimedia Commons,* http://commons.wikimedia.org. **66**–Dieter Noack and Lilian Noack, *The Daumier Register.* **67**–National Lottery, Heritage Lottery Fund, "Capital-Build Or Refurbishment Projects," *National Lottery, Heritage Lottery Fund,* http://www.hlf.org.uk. **67**–Canadian Heritage, Government of Canada, "Acknowledgement and Disclaimer Guide for Organizations Receiving Funding for Capital Projects Through the Building Communities Through Arts and Heritage Program," *Canadian Heritage, Government of Canada,* http://www.pch.gc.ca/eng/1281381118205.

TREYF?

treyf, adj. [Yiddish]—not kosher, unclean.

Treyf—unusual books of an indeterminate type, sort of story-picture remix books for people who can't stomach any more schmaltzy *Chicken Soup for the Soul.* Treyf is cooked up using texts and images collected from various sources, usually obsessively related to one or more themes, and then recombined through a process of highly subjective editing, ordering and juxtaposition.

"Strange and clever." — Globe & Mail

"Funny, but deep." — Umbrella

"Is this a new form of discourse in step with its multivalent, chaotic times, or just an excuse for intellectual laziness? Only the author knows for sure." — Canadian Architect

www.treyf.com
keep refrigerated

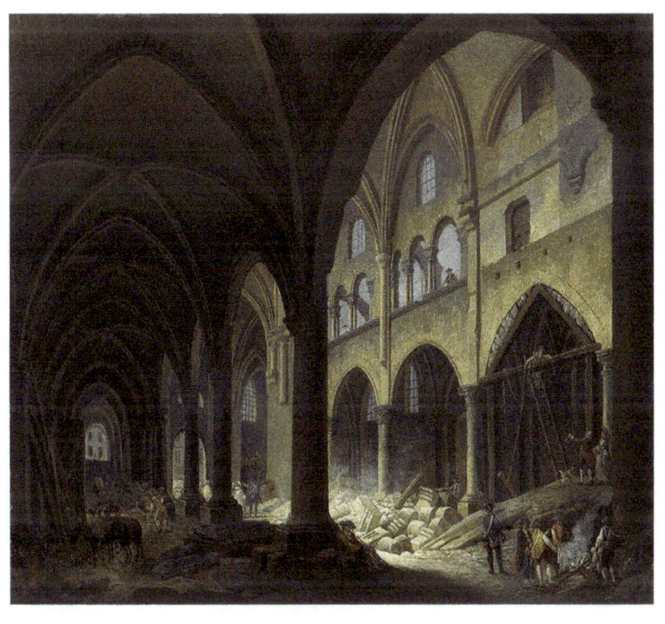

Pierre-Antoine Demachy, *Demolition of L'eglise des Saints Innocents, Paris*

Indistinctly signed and dated lower left,
oil on panel, 49.2 by 63.2 cm, circa 1787

ACKNOWLEDGEMENTS

For building projects, public acknowledgement means that there must be visible signs in place in public areas throughout the life of your grant contract with us, both during construction and after completion.

Acknowledging funding from us shows your success in gaining our support, and should begin as soon as work gets underway. While building or ground work funded by us is underway, you should acknowledge our support clearly so that the work taking place can be understood by the passing public.

National Lottery, Heritage Lottery Fund, *Capital-Build or Refurbishment Projects*

Please note: This is the general acknowledgement policy. Please see sections 6.0 to 13.0 below for more specific acknowledgement options.

The following disclaimer should also appear directly after the funding acknowledgement clause on all publications and websites (except when use of the short form funding clause has been pre-approved):

The opinions expressed in this publication (or on this website) do not necessarily reflect those of the Department of Canadian Heritage.

Canadian Heritage, Government of Canada, *Acknowledgement and Disclaimer Guide for Organizations Receiving Funding for Capital Projects Through the Building Communities Through Arts and Heritage Program*

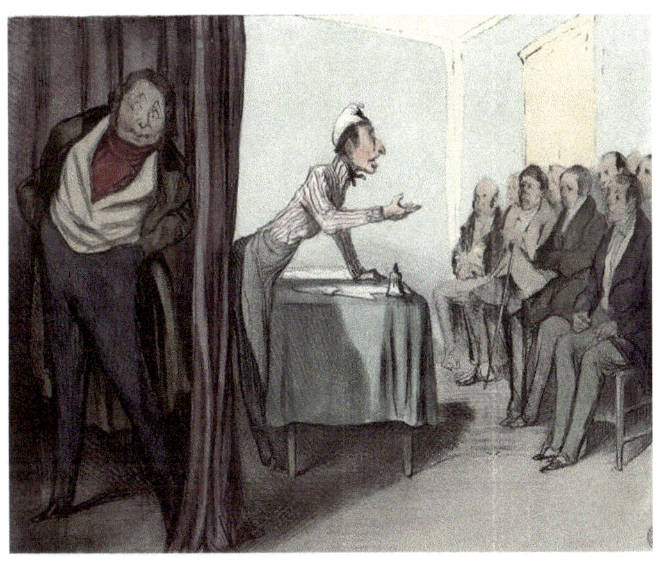

My dear Stockholders,

The founder of the firm, Mr. Macaire, has resigned from his post of director. The position in which he has left the business is as follows: Share capital, 800'000 Fr. Expenditure on posters, classified advertisements, handbills and newspaper articles, 400'000 Fr. Purchases of economy furnaces, matches, saucepans and top quality carrots, 400'000 Fr. Remaining in hand, 400'000 zeros. In other words, our funds have been cooked, we've consumed them all. Rather than putting Paris in the stew, we have eaten our own soup and if we don't put some spice in the eating, the pot will boil over. (a new investment of ... is then voted with unanimity ...)

Honoré Daumier, *Le Charivari,* 4 June 1837

www.ingramcontent.com/pod-product-compliance
Ingram Content Group UK Ltd.
Pitfield, Milton Keynes, MK11 3LW, UK
UKHW021835270726
14058UKWH00002B/162

9 781927 923054